A WOLF AND A JACKAL

By the same author

And a Wolf was Born

A Wolf and a Jackal

CLIFFORD H. FRY

ROBERT HALE · LONDON

© Clifford H. Fry 1995
First published in Great Britain 1995

ISBN 0 7090 5727 X

Robert Hale Limited
Clerkenwell House
Clerkenwell Green
London EC1R 0HT

The right of Clifford H. Fry to be identified as
author of this work has been asserted by him
in accordance with the Copyright, Designs and
Patents Act 1988.

Photoset in North Wales by
Derek Doyle & Associates, Mold, Clwyd.
Printed and bound in Great Britain by
WBC Book Manufacturers Limited,
Bridgend, Mid-Glamorgan.

Author's Note

While this is essentially a work of fiction, it will be understood that the battle of the First Bull Run of 1861 is a well documented fact of American history, as were Generals McDowell, Beauregard and George Jackson whose defence of Bull Run earned him the famous nickname, 'Stonewall'.

However, the characters of Eli Kyle, Nathaniel Kyle and Jason McKendrick (*Concho*) depicted in the battle are, as far as I am aware, the product of my own imagination.

If by some freak chance I have selected real names of people who took part in this historic battle, I sincerely apologize to their descendants.

Clifford H. Fry

My grateful thanks to Elisabeth Roberts
for her unstinting help along the way.

To my wife Enid
(who had to read everything at least twice).

ONE

Although it was barely nine o'clock in the morning, the pitiless sun caused the desert sands to reflect a shimmer of heat around the stationary wagon, giving it a trembling mirage-like effect.

The two horses stood hip-shot with heads hanging in tired submission to the heat, nudging each other gently into a new position beside the wagon as the sun moved around it attempting to deprive the listless horses of what little shade there was.

Nathaniel's heart was heavy as he paused with his two wooden buckets filled with the scummy dirty water he'd carried from the sinks nearby.

There was less water in the sinks today, two more days and his water supply for the horses would dry up completely.

The horses whickered a welcome; they could smell the water but were reluctant to leave the scant shade of the wagon in order to obtain it.

Nathaniel's blue eyes crinkled as laughter lines pulled at them. 'God-damn if you ain't the laziest broncs I ever did see,' he chuckled in a deep Texas drawl, as he put the two buckets beside the wagon and reached into the fodder box for some hay which he scattered beside the two animals.

The horses pushed forward nuzzling the hay almost indifferently before starting to munch away at the feed.

'I was beginning to think you were waiting for a knife and fork,' he told them as he reached for his tobacco bag and papers and began making a quirley.

He slumped almost dejectedly against the side of the wagon as he rolled the smoke.

His broad-brimmed stetson was tilted forward to protect his eyes from the sun's glare as he scanned his back-trail, checking for the slightest sign of movement.

He leaned forward over the remains of the breakfast fire, selected a glowing piece of wood and sucked life into the cigarette.

He felt the acrid tang of the smoke in his throat so he threw the stick back into glowing coals, his eyes continuing their patient search.

Nathaniel Kyle was six-four, a lean, tough one hundred and ninety pounds, tall even for a Texan. His careful search continued until he had finished his smoke and had pinched it out, then he stood up, a signal to his wife that he was satisfied.

'No company then, Nathan?' asked Sarah from behind the wagon's backcloth.

'None I can see, gal,' he replied. 'Which don't mean damn all of course.'

'I happen to think it does,' replied Sarah. 'We've bin travelling this way for a fair few years now and your eyes ain't let us down yet.'

She pulled back the heavy tarp sheet and jumped nimbly from the wagon. Sarah was a short, slim, bird-like creature and her prematurely greying hair, pulled back from her face into a tight bun heightened the illusion. Her face seemed sharp, somehow rather severe. The constant worry of the man somewhere on their back-trail and the perpetual fear of his vow to kill her husband had cut deep worry lines into her face, making her seem much older than her thirty years. But the moment she smiled, her whole face came alive and her real age showed through.

Nathaniel had a half smile on his face as he watched her kick the remains of the fire together then fetch some sticks from the tailgate box.

The years of running showed on him too, making creases in his face that had no right to be there.

In no time at all Sarah had a small bright fire blazing.

Satisfied, she turned to face him, hands on hips with her head tilted to one side as she smiled into his face.

He grinned in return. He always did, he thought absently, he just plain couldn't help it.

Sarah reached up and caught his face in her almost too tiny hands, drawing him down to her. 'Don't look so glum, honey,' she murmured. 'He won't ever part us.'

She kissed him firmly. 'I'll make some coffee, that should do the trick.'

'We've been running a long time now, Sarah. One day I'm gonna have to stop. Look at us, we've had no chance to settle. You've had no home except this lousy wagon, no children to rock or wean and for what!'

'Hush now Nathan,' she murmured, placing a finger over his mouth. 'You've got me! You'll always have me, you *know* that. But you can't lie in wait to kill your own brother, Nathan. God would never forgive you.'

'Then I should face him man to man with a gun in my hand.'

'I think you can do most things you set your mind to, Nathan,' she replied, 'but do you honestly think you'd have a chance against *him*? He's a bounty hunter and a killer while you're trying your best to be a preacher.'

She kissed him again and stepped quickly away. 'Coffee,' she said firmly.

'He'll never give up,' replied Nathan sadly, shaking his head. 'You don't know him as I do.'

'Coffee,' she repeated, lifting the blackened pot from its hook, filling it from the large water barrel fixed to the side of the wagon and setting it on the glowing coals.

Nathaniel watched her his mind in a turmoil. Yet part of him still noticed how clean and neat she always managed to keep herself. She never seemed to get dirty or grubby. The gingham dress she was wearing could not be cleaner if she'd just bought it. Her hair was always so neat and tidy....

A movement tagged the corner of his eye; he was instantly alert.

'Get up slowly, Sarah, and get into the wagon. Gently now,' he cautioned as he leaned over to pat one of the horses. 'Put my rifle in the usual place.'

Sarah was already moving. She called some quip as she climbed nonchalantly over the tailgate and eased the tarp cover almost closed while Nathaniel crouched below the opening and began to roll a smoke.

Seemingly concentrating on the quirley his eyes flicked quickly over the spot where he thought he had seen the movement.

He had been right! There was a slight lift in the contour of the ridge that had not been there before.

He allowed his eyes to wander from the mark. It did not do to stare at one point for too long, it was too easy to notify a stalker that he'd been spotted.

Nathan finished rolling the cigarette giving it the final one-handed twist.

It gave him a reason to move, and that might not be a bad idea he thought wryly. Whoever was up there could be drawing a bead on him right now.

The thought made him nervous as he leaned forward. Removing the coffeepot he selected a glowing piece of wood from the fire.

There was a minute flash of sunlight on glass as the watcher followed his movement. A telescope! Not an Indian then, he mused. Could it be that his half-brother had caught up with him at last?

His hand shook slightly as he touched the brand to his smoke.

Nathan threw the branch back into the fire and turned as if to sit on the ground with his back to a wheel.

In one swift movement he twisted his legs and rolled under the protection of the wagon as the whine of a heavy calibre bullet spanged off the steel rim.

A second quickly followed kicking dust into Nathan's face as he squirmed away and rolled to the centre of the vehicle. A third and fourth followed, the special boom telling him it was a Sharps.

Nathan waited patiently, out of reach of the probing bullets as Sarah unlatched and lifted the trap in the floor and Nathan quickly scrambled through, replacing the trap.

'Keep low, gal,' he muttered as he crawled across the floor and lifted the heavy timber side boards into position to give their meagre protection added height.

'Is it Eli d'you think?' asked Sarah.

'Not Eli,' he muttered. 'That's a Sharps; Eli hates 'em.'

The side boards slotted into the lower boards by means of upright flat iron bars and straps. Now that they were in position they could sit on the floor of the wagon and still be protected, unless a stray bullet should find one of the rifle ports of course.

Nathan slid across the floor to collect his Henry rifle.

'Now it ain't quite so one-sided, honey,' he muttered, 'If he shows me a whisker I'll damn well clip it for him.'

'You sound nothing like any preacher I ever heard,' groused Sarah, checking her own carbine. 'Downright bloody-minded if you ask me.'

There had been no further shots from the unknown marksman.

'He's after the wagon and horses,' grunted Nathan thoughtfully.

'You think so?'

'Know so; otherwise he'd have killed 'em by now.'

'So he's got us pinned down, huh?'

'Only till nightfall.'

'Then you go gallivanting, I suppose.'

'You suppose right,' he replied.

'Might be more than one out there, Nathan.'

'Nope, don't reckon so. If there'd bin more than one they would have taken us from both sides at once. He was alone and unsure; that's why he left it so late to try.'

The day dragged slowly on and the heat within the wagon gradually built to unbearable proportions.

They heard no more from the gunman, so each took a turn to slip through the trapdoor and lie in the cool shade under the wagon while the other kept a constant watch through the loopholes in the boards.

It was late afternoon when Nathan decided that it was safe to have a short sleep.

'Keep a good look out, Sarah,' he told her. 'I'll get some shut-eye now so that I'll be fresh for tonight.'

Sarah nodded as she handed him some left-over soda cakes.

'Best have something to chew on,' she muttered. 'You always dream on an empty stomach.'

'I dream anyway,' Nathan grinned, as he took the

cakes and slid through the trapdoor. 'I think he's packed it in for now but I've bin wrong before.'

'You tellin' me,' replied Sarah dryly.

'Don't worry, hon, just close the trap and keep the carbine handy, call me when the sun goes down.'

With the trap closed, he stretched out on his back and placed his rifle beside him.

The rifle reminded him, as always, of that other rifle so long ago. Of a killing so awful that his half-brother was still following him with murder in his heart. Nathan's eyes slowly closed as his mind drifted back in time....

TWO

Nathaniel could hear his mother calling him for supper. He could tell by the sound of her voice that she'd been crying again.

She always seemed to be crying these days he thought sadly.

His elder brother Eli stuck his head into the barn. 'Didn't you hear your ma call you?' he growled, in a surly voice.

'Yeah I'm comin', Eli,' Nathan replied.

'Then move it or I'll kick yore ass just like my pa kicks hers.'

Nathan's lips trembled. He could never understand why Eli disliked him so much or why he always said *my* pa not *our* pa and if Nathan should make a mistake and say '*our* pa' Eli would beat him unmercifully.

From the scraps of conversation he had overheard Nathan realized that Eli was a half-breed, and that his mother had been a Pawnee Indian. Though what difference that made Nathan found difficult to understand, but perhaps he'd understand more as he got older. Being barely fifteen seemed to have a lot of disadvantages. Whereas Eli, who was eighteen, seemed to know everything.

Nathan was startled from his thoughts as Eli cuffed

him around the ear with enough force to send him tumbling to the floor.

'Don't stand there day-dreamin',' he snarled, kicking Nathan on the muscle of his upper leg. 'Get a bloody move on.'

Nathan scrambled to his feet limping badly from the kick. 'You had no call to do that, Eli,' he protested. 'I was just comin'.'

Eli stalked menacingly towards Nathan, and although Eli was stocky Nathan suddenly realized that he was outgrowing Eli.

For the first time in his life Nathan rebelled. He clenched his fists and faced his elder brother.

Eli paused, a shadow of doubt passing across his face. 'You defying me, Nathan?' he queried almost disbelievingly. 'I'll kick the living shit out of you, little brother.'

'Ma said not to swear,' replied Nathan defiantly.

Eli pointed to the barn door, his voice rising in anger. 'Git while you can still stand,' he almost screeched.

Nathan was amazed at his own temerity. 'I'll go when I'm good 'n ready,' he muttered sullenly.

With a howl of anger Eli launched himself at Nathan, kicking and punching like a madman.

Shocked at the onslaught Nathan could only wrap his muscular arms around his brother to try to contain the madness.

In doing so the strength of Eli's charge forced Nathan into a quick turn making him release Eli.

Nathan was amazed to see his brother crash into the side of the barn with enough force to knock him flat on his back where he lay without moving.

Nathan was instantly contrite as he ran to his brother and knelt beside him.

'I'm sorry, Eli,' he muttered brokenly. 'I didn't mean to hurt you.'

He put out his hand to touch Eli's face.

Quite suddenly Nathan was screaming in agony as Eli grabbed his middle finger and bent it backwards; his screams reached a crescendo as the bone gave an awful crack and Nathan fainted.

Nathan seemed to hear his mother calling his name from a great distance but it was wrong somehow because his mother never called him anything but Nathaniel and this voice was calling Nathan.

The call became louder and he shook himself awake with a hoarse cry of '*Ma!*'

He was streaming with sweat as he stared uncomprehendingly at the face of his wife peering through the trap opening.

'It's time Nathan,' she murmured. 'Are you all right?'

'Yeah, yeah, I'm OK, honey,' he muttered wiping his arm across his face to remove some of the moisture.

'Dreaming again?' Sarah asked worriedly.

''Fraid so, hon. What time is it?'

'Sun's down and the moon ain't showed itself yet. About right if you intend to move across all that open ground.'

Nathan picked up his rifle as Sarah passed him his hand-gun and holster.

'Thanks Sarah,' he muttered. 'Usual thing, love. Keep the trapdoor shut and keep low. Any movement out there stick the Greener out and let 'em have it. Usual signal when I get back. OK?'

'I know, Nathan. We've done it all before. Now git before the moon makes it as light as day out there.'

Nathan slipped from under the wagon and stood up

A Wolf and a Jackal

in the deep shadow. He quickly strapped on his gunbelt as one of the horses gave a gentle whicker of welcome.

They were at ease, a sure sign that there were no strangers in the near vicinity.

Crouching low he hurried directly towards the place where he had seen that tell-tale flash of sunlight on glass, it was a safe bet that the man would no longer be there but the tracks would be.

He slipped silently over the ridge and waited for the moon to come up. Within moments the huge disc lifted above the horizon bathing the whole area in its soft, silvery light.

The wagon stood out. A stark contrast to the flat planes of desert and hard pan.

Nathan carefully quartered the area searching for the intruder but nothing moved in the silvery light.

Nathan had judged the position exactly. To his left he could clearly see the disturbance where the man had lain while studying the wagon. He could also see the footmarks in the side of the ridge.

Nathan began to follow the outgoing trail, sure now that he was dealing with a white man. No Indian would have left such an obvious trail.

Soon Nathan came to the place where the man had left his horse. The tracks told him that the horse was limping badly.

Nathan's alarm bells began to ring. The man needed another horse so where else would he go but to the wagon?

Nathan began to run then, back up the ridge and over the top in a mad dash for the wagon. The crafty sonofabitch had used the same darkness to get to the wagon where Sarah was waiting, alone!

On the heels of the thought he heard three rapid

shots; it registered that they were the light, sharp cracks of Sarah's carbine, followed by the booming roar of the Sharps.

In desperation Nathan fired into the air. It would let Sarah know that he was coming as fast as he could. True it would also alert the attacker but it might make him decide to break off the engagement.

He heard the Sharps boom again and instinctively ducked as a whisper of displaced air passed close above his head.

Nathan continued his headlong run. Either this *hombre* was an excellent shot or it had been a lucky one he thought grimly.

There was another three rapid cracks from the carbine.

Sarah was still in the fight he thought gratefully. She'd have his number by this time.

Another shot from the Sharps had him diving to the ground for protection.

He could not return the fire for fear of hitting the horses which were still in the deep shadow of the wagon.

As if in answer to his silent prayer the two horses suddenly scattered into the moonlight.

Nathan could only assume that the attacker had tried to capture one of them but in so doing had frightened them both.

The stock of the Henry rifle slipped into his shoulder and he began to lay a pattern of fire into the shadowed area. Sarah's carbine also opened up in concert.

It was too much for the unknown man to stomach.

There was a loud curse and flurry of hooves as the attacker rode away on his badly limping mount.

Nathan sent three shots close to the fleeing man but the moonlight coupled with the oddly moving horse made him a difficult target and he was reluctant to waste ammunition hoping for a lucky shot.

'You OK Sarah?' he called, 'I'm comin' in.'

'Come ahead, Nathan. Best bring the broncs in close and tie 'em to the wagon for tonight; that varmint might just fancy trying his luck a second time.'

That's my gal, he thought wryly. Just been in a shooting war and up she pops as chipper as ever and even more bossy if that was possible.

The remainder of the night was passed in fitful sleep, but at first light they were both up and around as if nothing had happened and while Nathan took the horses for a final long drink at the sinks, Sarah lit the fire and started cooking breakfast.

At the sinks Nathan could clearly see where their attacker had spent the night but he too was long gone.

Nathan continued to stare at the trail left by the limping pony. 'By my calculation he's heading straight for the Dust Bowl,' he muttered. 'Nothing out there for many a long mile, and with a limping bronc he could be dead by nightfall and I don't just mean the hoss either.'

Nathan knew that while the Sioux would probably ignore the odd white man as beneath contempt, the much more warlike tribes of Pawnee or Northern Cheyenne were a different matter.

Nathan's only reason for travelling these dangerous trails was to try to coax Eli back among his own people, where he might decide to give up the long chase and finally settle down with his own tribe.

THREE

It was some three hours later that Nathan heard the distant crackle of gunfire.

It was so faint that he halted the wagon in order to listen.

They were about to move off again when Sarah stopped Nathan with a hand on his arm.

'Gunshots right enough,' she muttered. 'How far away d'you reckon?'

'Can't rightly say, gal; sound can travel an awful long way out here.' After some thought he continued, 'Reckon it might be the *hombre* from last night in trouble somewhere up by the Dust Bowl.'

He flipped the traces and the horses plodded forward once more.

'If it is and he's got trouble I hope it's fatal,' replied Sarah waspishly.

'Now that's no way for a preacher's wife to be talking is it?' he chided.

'Humph,' replied Sarah, inelegantly. 'D'you suppose the Indians would notice?'

'Nope.'

'So who else is there out there?'

The banter continued backwards and forwards but it was only a cover.

A Wolf and a Jackal

Both were listening to the spasmodic crack of rifle fire as the day wore on until Nathan silently pointed his whip at a mound of rocks.

The wagon had been following the tracks of the semi-lame horse for quite some time but here was where the tracks ended.

The horse was stretched out beside the rocks where last night's raider had left it. The animal was not dead but very close to it.

Nathan unclipped his rifle from inside the wagon and passed the lines to Sarah before stepping down cautiously and carefully looking around.

Sarah tied off the lines and slipped down the opposite side of the wagon.

The Greener was on the footplate and it took but a second to point the lethal double barrels across the footplate to cover the rocks.

This was a routine they had practised many times together in their travels across the new territories while attempting to outwit Eli Kyle.

Remembering the raider's uncanny accuracy with the Sharps, Nathan moved swiftly sideways to make a much wider angle of fire in case the man was still around.

A quick search, however, revealed the man's tracks, still heading in the general direction of the Dust Bowl.

Nathan waved for Sarah to come in.

'He's heading for hell in a hurry,' he muttered as she approached. 'No way he can walk all the way to Casa Verde, so I reckon he'll be making for the same place as us.'

'You mean he's heading for Peaceful?'

'I reckon,' replied Nathan succinctly.

'Perhaps he heard the shooting up ahead and is hoping to pick up a spare bronc,' answered Sarah. 'All that gunfire must mean someone's the worse for wear.'

'Could be,' agreed Nathan. 'Guess I'd better put the cayuse out of its misery.

'Can't risk a shot with all that gunfire up ahead,' he explained, as he drew his Bowie. 'If we can hear them they will sure-God hear us.'

Sarah nodded her understanding. 'If the creature *has* to die it might as well provide us with a decent supper. We could also dry out some of the meat for pemmican, it ain't venison but it would do a turn.'

'Steaks then?' asked Nathan.

Sarah nodded. 'You do the butchering, I'll unload the wagon and set the fire. Keep a sizeable piece back for boiling too, I'll set it in the pot to cook overnight, make a nice change.'

Nathan chuckled as he walked away.

What a woman, he thought. Nothing seemed to faze her.

They had heard no shots for some time so it was tacitly decided that they would spend the coming night tucked up safely in the rocks.

They had enjoyed their meal and had set the pot to simmer as the moon came up, once again casting its bright silver light over everything, softening the scenery and cooling the ground.

Suddenly they heard a flurry of gunshots. A double shot-gun blast followed by more shots.

'Hand-guns,' muttered Nathan automatically.

'And a Greener,' responded Sarah.

Nathan nodded, still listening.

There was a long pause then two more shots rang out. 'Rifle,' announced Nathan with conviction. 'That's some fight going on up there.'

'Glad we decided to stop here,' remarked Sarah. 'In a

way that raider did us a big favour.'

'And fed us to boot,' grinned Nathan.

They heard no more shots so they decided to get an early night and make some progress before sun-up the following day.

It was still dark when Nathan hitched the horses to the wagon while Sarah packed away the last of the breakfast dishes.

The moon had given them light to prepare and eat their breakfast but now it had dropped below the horizon ready for the dawning.

'Keep a weather eye open, Sarah,' Nathan muttered, as he clucked the horses into motion. 'We're heading in the direction of that mess of shooting we heard last night.'

'We could move a little further north, Nathan.'

'It would put us awful close to the Black Hills,' responded Nathan. 'It would also add three days before we get to water, so as I see it there's just no other way to go.'

'If you say so,' replied Sarah as the sun climbed into the sky behind them and began to warm the earth once again.

They were planning to skirt the edge of the Dust Bowl before dropping down towards Cherry Creek and the badlands beyond but as they approached a small coulée Sarah heard a horse whicker.

She placed a warning hand on Nathan's arm.

'I heard it,' he muttered as he passed the traces to her and took his rifle from its clip. 'Take it easy now, gal.'

With a quick pat on her arm he slipped from the wagon and moved swiftly ahead until he came to a rock-strewn clearing.

A palomino pony was moving restlessly backwards

and forwards in front of a body lying in the sand. Its whickering and snuffling was all that was preventing the vultures from venturing too close.

Nathan raised a warning hand to Sarah.

She stopped the wagon, tied the traces and picked up the shot-gun before climbing down and advancing slowly towards her spouse.

By this time Nathan could see that there was more than one cadaver in the clearing so the buzzards were finding plenty to eat without going too close to the horse.

Nathan waved his hand at Sarah again, telling her to stay back as he slowly made his way into the clearing.

He threw some rocks at the birds to drive them off but they didn't go far.

'Come ahead as far as the rock,' he called quietly. 'But stay there. There's two more bodies further in and they ain't a pretty sight.'

Sarah followed Nathan's instructions and moved to where he had been standing.

She could see the pony and the apparently dead man beside it. After a quick glance she turned to watch as Nathan approached the other bodies, her eyes scanning the rocks around him for signs of danger.

She no longer considered the man lying beside the restive horse a threat and neither did Nathan. He was more interested in the other two.

One had been killed with his guns in his hands. A pair of ornate pearl-handled Colts lay beside him in mute testimony.

The other had been shot from the front, with six bullets around the heart in an area no bigger than the palm of Nathan's hand.

'Some mean shooting,' he muttered, as he hunkered

A Wolf and a Jackal

down to study the sawn-off shot-gun fixed to the man's leather belt with a metal swivel.

The distinctive snick of a six-gun brought to full cock made the hairs on the back of his neck prickle.

You *fool! you didn't check the one beside the horse*! his brain screamed, as he twisted frantically sideways, desperately trying to bring his rifle to bear, but knowing it was already too late.

Sarah saw the sudden frantic urgency in Nathan and twisted quickly towards the threat also, trying to turn the shot-gun.

She was barely in time to see the man beside the horse.

He was still lying almost prone, but now there was a revolver in his hand and it was pointing towards her man.

Sarah screamed a desperate 'No!' as the hammer fell and the gun roared its song of death....

FOUR

Eli Kyle studied the featureless wastes around him dispassionately as his horse plodded towards the town somewhere ahead.

He had been diverted from his search for his half-brother because of his ever present need for the funds to continue, so he had once again reverted to the role of bounty hunter.

Eli was good at it! Once on the trail of a fugitive he would stick like a burr under a saddle until they just plain gave up.

Most of the reward dodgers said 'Dead or Alive' but to Eli's way of thinking they were much easier to take back dead so why do it the hard way?

He'd even had a few surrender, but he soon discovered that if he pretended to be careless most men would try to escape sooner or later.

From then on they were strapped face down across their saddles, and what was more they didn't even need feeding.

Being a halfbreed Pawnee Eli knew the value of superstition and he cultivated that fear in everything he did.

He dressed all in black. His saddle and bridle were black as was his horse. He preferred the flat-crowned, wide-brimmed black Amish-type hat rather than the traditional stetson while his cut-away black coat and trousers made him look like an undertaker.

A suggestion of a smile pulled at his wide Slavic face as he thought of the newspaper cutting he'd collected from the last town he'd visited: THE ANGEL OF DEATH screamed the banner headlines.

Death rode into our little town yesterday and three men died.
Death left this morning, praise the Lord.

Eli Kyle wore two guns around his waist but they were not a matching pair.

His right-hand gun was an 1856 Starr percussion .44, a gun he could draw with the speed of a striking snake. He'd cherished the weapon ever since Bull Run when he'd stolen it from his own superior officer.

He had stolen the holster also, together with everything else the unfortunate man had possessed.

The other gun, a Le Mat nine-shot percussion revolver with an underslung second barrel firing a devastating 20 gauge shot-gun cartridge really struck terror into the men he hunted. In fact it was so deadly at close quarters that it was nicknamed the Grapeshot Pistol and had been greatly feared by both sides in the Civil War.

One day Eli hoped to see Nathaniel Kyle standing within fifteen feet of that lethal shot-gun barrel as he squeezed the trigger.

The Spencer sniper's rifle snugged in the saddle boot completed Eli's formidable armoury.

Eli had travelled a long way over several years hoping to kill his hated half-brother.

He had even joined the Union army as a scout when he'd discovered that Nathaniel had joined the Confederacy.

He fought in the first Bull Run under General McDowell in July of '61 and had missed killing Nathaniel by a hair as their positions were overrun by the Confederates under Beauregard and Jackson.

Since then their paths had almost crossed several times. At the end of the war Eli had continued his quest.

From Wichita Falls to Kansas City, over to Sioux Falls and up to Big Stone Lake. He'd crossed the Missouri twice, once in Nebraska and once in North Dakota but now he was about to enter a small township near the Cheyenne River in the South Dakotas.

A town called Sellick.

Eli pulled the reward dodger from inside his coat and spread it out.

The worn dodger proclaimed that a Jackson and Harvey Murdock were wanted in Kansas for cattle-rustling. The dodger was over a year old but as far as Eli was concerned it still held good.

They were probably a couple of dirt farmers who had stolen nothing in their lives, but had started ploughing some big cattleman's land; it happened all the time.

Eli shrugged, he didn't give a damn whether they were guilty or not. They represented $1,000 and that was all he needed to know.

Eli rode steadily on through the heat until the scattering of buildings shimmering in the sunlight gradually took shape.

A rough board nailed to a stake driven into the packed earth had the legend SELLICK printed on it. It looked as if some smart alec had tried to dot the 'I' with a bullet hole at least a dozen times without success.

A Wolf and a Jackal

Something that might have been a smile flitted across his face. If that was the accepted standard of marksmanship he'd have no trouble, he thought absently.

Eli drew rein at a building with the word MARSHAL over the door.

A middle-aged man was leaning against the building whittling on a piece of wood. His hat was tipped over his eyes and there was a badge on his denim shirt. He was chewing industriously on a chaw of cut plug.

'You the marshal?' asked Eli, from the saddle.

The man pushed his hat to the back of his balding head. ''Breed huh?' he replied, spitting a gob of tobacco juice at the horse's feet as he returned to his whittling.

'Asked you a question, mister.'

The man looked up again as if Eli was a tick that was beginning to annoy him.

He tapped the badge with his knife. 'This ain't fer target practice, mister, an' it says sheriff. Can't you read or shall I send up a smoke signal?'

He must have thought it was funny because he started to guffaw, and his belly started to dance in tune.

He pointed his paring knife at Eli. 'Good 'un that, smoke signals, get it?'

The smile slowly died as Eli casually drew the Le Mat and pointed it at the badge.

'Wonder if I *can* hit it from here,' Eli speculated aloud, as he drew the hammer to full cock.

The man gulped and swallowed his tobacco, his face reddened as he began to choke.

The gun disappeared, Eli slipped quickly from the saddle and began to pound the man enthusiastically on the back.

'Easy there, old son,' Eli laughed in a falsely friendly

tone. 'You're likely to choke to death eatin' tobacco like that.'

The man was struggling to get away from Eli, but he continued to pound away.

'Fer Christ's sake, pack it in,' spluttered the sheriff. 'You're likely to knock the brains out of me poundin' my back like that.'

'Naw,' reassured Eli. 'If I wanted to knock your brains out I'd be kicking your rear end, feller.'

He grabbed the unfortunate sheriff's arm and guided him into the office. Still retaining his hold he forced him behind his desk and sat him in the chair.

'Now, I'm gonna ask you one more time, are you the marshal or sheriff of this here county?'

'Sheriff,' the man grunted, still shocked at Eli's savagery. 'Marshal's out of town.'

'Good, now we're gettin' somewhere.' Eli slapped the reward dodgers in front of him. 'Are these still good?'

The man fiddled with them for a while then pushed them back to Eli. 'They ain't bin cancelled; so as far as I know they're still good.'

'So if I bring you the two men in alive or dead you'll pay the reward, yes?'

'That's what it says, so that's what I'll do, but yore a 'breed. The men around here won't like it you bein' a 'breed an' all.'

'You leave that to me, just get the money ready, understand?'

'Sure, sure I understand if you say so.'

'I do, so don't forget it. These two *hombres* are in your town right now, and unless I miss my guess I'll find 'em both in the saloon.'

'Ain't *my* town, I done told you. The marshal's out of town just now. I'm County Sheriff. Anyway you ain't allowed in the saloon; you're a 'breed.'

'So you keep saying. Now get the money, I'll be back.'

Eli Kyle strolled out on to the porch, hat tilted forward to protect his eyes.

He took a long, thin, black cheroot from his vest pocket, and pushed it into the corner of his mouth as he studied the saloon four places down on the opposite side of the street.

'Time to earn a year's pay,' he muttered, as he stepped off the sidewalk and made his slow deliberate way towards the saloon.

He flicked a match head with his thumbnail and lit the cheroot. Each movement was calculated and deliberate.

He paused by the batwings and stared into the darker interior, allowing his eyes to become accustomed to the inner gloom.

There were only a few people inside. Four were sitting at a table playing cards. Two more were seated in the far corner. Both had beer glasses in front of them.

Eli scanned the room again, the two in the corner were the most likely. He pushed open the batwings and slowly entered.

'What'll it be, mister?' asked the bartender cheerfully as he walked towards Eli. 'Beer? Whiskey? I—' His voice trailed off as he realized that Eli was a half-breed. 'Ain't no use you askin' for a drink in here, mister, we don't serve Indians, so best be on your way.'

'Didn't ask for a drink,' replied Eli evenly, as he began to stroll leisurely along the length of the bar. 'An I'll go when I'm ready; got some business to take care of first.'

The barman was quick to sense trouble. He bent double as his hands dipped quickly under the bar.

Eli's left hand moved also and the bartender found himself looking directly into the ominous muzzle of the

Le Mat now resting on the bar top, the bore of the shot-gun section looking like the mouth of a tunnel.

The bartender froze.

'Lift it out slow 'n easy,' Eli said evenly, without even looking at the man. 'Just place it on the bar top an' unload it.'

The barkeep did as he was told. He realized it was not a good day to die.

'That's fine; now just walk with me to the other end of the bar. If you've got another gun down there, don't get tempted. I don't want to kill you but believe me I will.'

'I believe you, mister,' muttered the bartender fervently as he walked slowly along on the opposite side of the bar keeping exactly level with the man in black.

They stopped at the end of the bar and Eli looked at the two young men sitting at the table in the corner. 'You happen to be the Murdock brothers?' he asked politely.

The two men looked at each other. One of them nodded. 'What about it?'

Eli pulled the dodgers from his vest pocket and dropped them on the table.

'You're under arrest,' he told them quietly. 'Let's just take a stroll down to the sheriff's office.'

The Le Mat was back in its holster and Eli had not attempted to draw his other weapon.

'Like hell we will,' growled one savagely. 'We didn't steal any damned steers; they just wanted us off our land. Well, we left, so that's it.'

'Sheriff tells me these dodgers are still good so I'm taking you in.'

The two men pushed the table away and stood up facing Eli their hands hovering over their guns.

'Only way we go out of here is feet first,' snarled the taller of the two.

A Wolf and a Jackal

'Your choice.' Eli shrugged. 'It's all the same to me, fellers.'

The two men's hands dipped as one but they were way too slow.

Eli's right hand was a blur. The Starr seemed to grow in his hand and the first shot punched a hole through the chest of the man on his right.

The gun flicked to the left. The second shot caught the other man under the chin, the bullet ploughed upwards through the top of his head pushing a fountain of blood and bone ahead of it.

Neither man had managed to lift their guns higher than their waist.

The barman stared disbelievingly at the carnage the 'breed had created in a matter of seconds.

'That was sheer bloody murder!' he ejaculated. 'They didn't stand one chance in a million.'

'Their choice,' replied Eli evenly, as he turned to look at the others. 'You all heard me, an' they drew first.'

The men around the card table began to mutter among themselves.

'Didn't stand a chance, ain't got no right bein' in here anyway,' growled another.

'Are we gonna let him get away with it?' asked a third.

The card players began to stand up as their tempers started to flare.

'Hey Joe,' asked the fourth, a very young cowboy. 'What kind of saloon d'you call this that you let 'breeds in here anyway?'

Joe remained silent as Eli pointed to the man who had just spoken.

'You, mister. You look like a right feisty *hombre*. Why don't you just step out here away from yore friends so they don't get caught in any gunfire, an' show 'em just what you'd do if you were Joe.'

The man was caught and he realized it. The others had been allowed to say their piece without trouble, and he'd enjoyed chiming in. He glanced desperately around him, but the others were avoiding any kind of eye contact.

Friends they might be, but just now he was a total stranger. Sudden death could leave a man kind of isolated.

He could feel a trickle of sweat running down his back but it had nothing to do with the heat of the day.

The young man tried to move, but his legs wouldn't obey. He was only eighteen and he didn't want to die. He felt an ominous warmth as he urinated, and more sweat began to run down his face.

'C'mon, sonny,' taunted Eli, 'step out an' show 'em what Joe should do.'

Joe had been slowly reaching for the second shot-gun under the counter. He could see that the half-breed was concentrating on the kid.

The barkeep lifted the gun very slowly and began to turn it towards the 'breed.

It would cut the man in half from this distance, he thought as he slipped his finger over the double triggers.

Joe looked up in time to see the Le Mat pointing at him.

As if in a dream he saw the shot-gun barrel on the Le Mat belch flame and smoke. He felt a searing pain in his chest as he crashed into the bottles behind the bar where he died in his own booze.

Eli had not taken his eyes off the men in front of him.

'See what happens when folks don't use their common sense?' he asked evenly. 'They turn into gutless wonders.

'Now, mister,' he continued to the thoroughly frightened young cowboy. 'D'you want to take up where the barkeep left off?'

A Wolf and a Jackal

The young man shook his head dumbly.

'Good, that's showin' sense. Now I'm goin' across to see the sheriff. Why don't you boys help yourselves to a drink on the house? I don't think the barkeep will object. You might even call it a wake in his honour – for being one dumb sonofabitch.'

Eli stepped around the men and walked backwards towards the batwings, pausing for a second to check that no one was waiting for him before stepping quickly out into the sunlight.

Eli reloaded his guns as he walked casually across to the sheriff's office but his eyes were alert for any sign of trouble.

The sheriff was still slouched in the marshal's chair when Eli stepped into the office.

'That gunfire mean you finished your business here?' he grunted sourly.

'You're one thousand dollars in debt,' replied Eli succinctly. 'Oh, an' one other small thing. The barkeep decided to play hero; the part didn't suit him so you'll be needing another barkeep.'

'Joe is a good man,' argued the sheriff.

'No, Joe *was* a good man,' corrected Eli. 'But not good enough; he had the drop but couldn't cut the mustard.'

The man in black picked up the money from the desk.

'Nice to know you had enough faith in my ability to draw the money like I asked, Sheriff,' he said quietly, as he stuffed the money in his pocket and turned to leave.

'One day someone just might come looking for you like that, mister,' growled the sheriff, anger pushing him.

Eli was casually scanning the Wanted posters on the wall. He collected two and stuffed them in his vest.

'They're welcome to try,' replied Eli without heat. 'But

I should try to make sure it isn't *you*, feller. See you around.'

'You leaving town now?' queried the sheriff hopefully.

Eli paused at the door. 'Just gonna collect some supplies from the store an' a mule to carry it. Why?'

'Sooner you go the sooner this town's gonna settle down. I don't want any trouble an' they might try to take you, mister.'

'Tell 'em not to get *too* ambitious, it could damage their health. *Adios*.'

Eli Kyle walked slowly to his horse and swung aboard.

The dry goods store was a few blocks from the livery stable where he managed to purchase a mule. The owner didn't seem interested in bargaining with Eli, and took the first price he offered.

It was the same at the dry goods store. Shopkeepers were usually a garrulous lot, but Eli was served in total silence. He could feel the animosity in the man's every movement.

It was obvious that the news had spread around the town like wildfire, and it seemed worse to the townsfolk because the men had been killed by a half-breed.

Eli knew that if they'd had the courage, neither the hostler nor the man in front of him would even consider serving him.

He shrugged as he carried his purchases outside and strapped them to the mule. Eli tied the lead rein to his saddle, then mounted his black stallion.

As he rode slowly past the bunch of chastened men standing outside the saloon Eli glanced down at them. A look of intense hatred mixed with distaste, flitted across his broad Slavic face as he touched his spurs to the horse and single-footed out of town. Ready once again to take up the hunt for his half-brother.

FIVE

As the man lying beside the palomino fired the shot he fell back, once again lapsing into unconsciousness.

Nathaniel heard the whisper of death as the bullet passed within inches of his face.

There was a clatter of metal against rock behind him. He twisted quickly towards the sound, rifle coming up as he turned.

Sarah was as if turned to stone, half turned towards the man beside the restive palomino, yet aware of the clatter in the rocks. She was trying to assess which was the greatest danger to her man when a rifle fell from the rocks, followed by the body of a man.

Nathan stepped back startled as the body rolled down and finished up almost at his feet.

Sarah began to run then. She'd forgotten all the things they'd rehearsed together so many times in the past.

She'd been so terribly afraid in those few awful seconds that Nathan was about to die. She had to get to him. Feel his arms around her, positive and reassuring.

Nathan too forgot everything as he swept her charging body into his arms and swung her around in the giddy ecstasy of the moment.

Both were trembling as he set his tiny wife on her feet again.

Sarah looked at the body in disbelief. There was a bullet hole where the man's nose should be, and the back of his head had almost disintegrated.

'H-he didn't intend to kill you at all,' she muttered. 'An' I was about ready to give him both barrels.'

Nathan pointed to the Sharps rifle on the ground. 'Our ambusher Sarah,' he murmured. 'It's too big a coincidence for it not to be.'

'He was fixing to kill you, Nathan. That man over there saw it and shot him.'

'It was some shot too,' agreed Nathan as they moved by common consent towards the unconscious man.

The palomino pawed the ground and snorted restlessly as the two approached, but Sarah spoke soothingly to it.

Gradually the horse calmed down and Nathan was able to kneel beside the man.

There was blood all over his face from a head wound, and his bloodied shirt told of a second wound high on the right shoulder.

Nathan felt for a pulse. To his surprise he could feel it, weak and fluttery, but it was there.

'He's still alive, Sarah. Get some water and cloths, quickly now.'

Sarah needed no urging. Whatever this man had done, he'd saved their lives in his last conscious effort. Now it's our turn, she thought, as her feet flew over the ground.

In moments she was back with a bucket of water and a cloth. She crouched beside the man and began to wipe away the blood from his head and face.

'Why he's just a youngster!' she murmured in wonder. 'He can't be more than eighteen summers, Nathan. What has he done I wonder to be left to die like this?'

All the while, she had been carefully bathing the head wound, and having cleaned it she began gently probing.

'It's not deep. The bullet skimmed across the front of his skull. He's been very lucky indeed. Get the wagon, Nathan. If we can keep him alive for twenty-four hours, I think we might be able to save him.'

While Nathan left to fetch the wagon Sarah carefully slid her hand under the damaged shoulder. She could feel a bulge just under the skin where the bullet had almost broken through.

Skilful, sensitive fingers checked the shoulder. As far as she could tell there was no break.

She heard the rumble of the wagon as Nathan drove it into the clearing. Sarah waved, and he came hurrying over.

'Hold him up, Nathan, while I cut out the bullet. Best get it done while he's still out of it. Might even get time to put him in the wagon too.'

'Anything broken?' he queried, as he cut away the shirt.

Sarah shook her head. 'Better cauterize that shoulder wound before any infection begins. Let's get him into the wagon. I'll bathe him while you light a fire.'

Nathan passed his knife to Sarah then lifted the damaged shoulder high enough so that she could cut across the slight bulge. The bullet dropped into her waiting hand.

'He's one lucky young man,' she muttered.

'Lucky for us too,' agreed Nathan. 'If it hadn't been for him we'd be dead, Sarah.'

Together they managed to get the young man upright, then Nathan stooped to allow the inert body to fall face down across one broad shoulder.

While Sarah hurried ahead and climbed into the wagon, Nathan carried the young man across.

Once the young man was safely on the bed Nathaniel left to light the fire. He took a piece of steel rod with him, once it was cherry-red he'd pass it to Sarah who would seal the wound, but while the fire was doing its part he collected his rifle from beside the body of the ambusher, and began to give the place his undivided attention.

Nathan stared long and hard at the would-be killer but he could not recollect ever seeing him before so assumed that they had been the victims of a chance encounter.

The big beefy man he knew by the swivel sawn-off shot-gun fixed to his belt.

Parker Rivers was notorious and there were many reward dodgers out on him.

The other man wasn't difficult to place either. The pearl-handled guns set him apart, and because he and Rivers were together, the name of 'Bruce Kincaid' was an easy label to pin on him.

That gave rise to another problem, however. The kid in the wagon had been shot with a rifle which meant that there had to have been a fourth man here who was able to walk away from the gunfight.

His thoughts were interrupted by a loud groan from the wagon.

Sarah must be treating the wounds with some of his Scotch whisky. Nathan mentally hoped that the kid appreciated the sacrifice but he doubted it.

Nathan quickly collected all the guns, including the sawn-off from Parker Rivers' body and carried them back to the wagon.

'How's the iron?' asked Sarah.

'About ready. I'll hold him. You do it?'

Sarah nodded. 'Let's get it done, he won't be out for much longer.'

Nathan hurried to the fire, the rod was glowing; he

wrapped a piece of cloth around it before taking it from the fire and running to the wagon.

The boy screamed in agony as the rod was pressed to the shoulder wound. The young body arched with the searing pain before he collapsed once again into oblivion and the sweet sickly smell of burning flesh filled the wagon.

Sarah threw the iron out of the wagon and rapidly bandaged the shoulder, using the same frontier expertise that she had used to bandage the head wound.

With Nathan giving a hand they managed to make him reasonably comfortable, but he looked very pale and was barely breathing.

There was a red bandanna around the boy's neck and Sarah slowly untied it.

The breath hissed through her teeth as she saw the scar of rope burn and skin loss.

'It looks almost as if he's been hanged or cut,' she muttered, shocked.

'Both I'd say,' agreed Nathan. 'He must be one bad *hombre*, and that knife he carries around his neck isn't for paring his nails you can bet on that.'

'But he saved your life, Nathaniel, and for that I'd forgive him almost anything.'

Nathan drew Sarah to him as best he could in the confined space.

'Let's hope he makes it, gal; he might not be as bad as we think.'

'We've done the best we can, Nathan. I suggest we have a bite to eat and then move on towards Cherry Creek. The further we go before he starts feeling the pain the better. I don't know about you, my lad, but a cup of coffee would just about hit the spot right now.'

'OK I get the message,' grinned Nathan. 'You fish out

some of that hoss meat you boiled and I'll set the coffee pot.'

They had finished their hastily prepared meal and Nathan was leaning against the wagon his face set in a thoughtful frown.

'There had to be another *hombre* in this fight, Sarah, the one with a rifle. Wonder what happened to him?'

Sarah shrugged. 'Anyway he's long gone now, so I doubt if we'll ever know.'

SIX

Sanchos Alvarez had ridden away quickly from the coulée wearing his superstitions like a cloak.

Shooting Jeff Mason, the man he himself had nicknamed *El Lobo Diablo*, had not been an easy thing to do, but the temptation had been too much for his avaricious nature.

He had been a member of the notorious Kincaid gang, and he had watched Mason cut them all down one by one.

They had called him *El Diablo!* Yet he had forgiven the one remaining member for some reason best known to himself, so he, Sanchos Alvarez, was still alive by the grace of *El Diablo*, and now he had repaid Mason by killing him from cover.

And look what he had gained! his mind whispered insidiously. Now he had the money from the bank raid in Casa Verde, the provisions and the packhorse which the two dead outlaws had unwittingly provided, and he didn't have to share it with anyone.

Not that he would have minded sharing it with Senor Mason of course, but Sanchos knew that Mason would have taken the money back to Casa Verde and he could not allow that to happen.

This was his once-in-a-lifetime chance to be a rich

man and he had to grab it with both hands. He must not worry about Mason coming back to haunt him.

This time *El Lobo* was dead.

He was sure of it. For had he not fired the fatal bullets himself? And had he not also inspected his handiwork afterwards?

Why then was he so uneasy? he asked himself.

Sanchos had spent the balance of that night in a rocky niche. He had eaten well from the provisions Kincaid and Rivers had provided, but his sleep had been fragmented by dreams of *El Lobo*. A spectre rising from the floor with blood all over his face as he had last seen him in the arroyo.

Then he had watched the dead man climb blindly on that devil horse and start following his tracks.

Sanchos rose early and was riding towards Cherry Creek long before dawn.

The Mexican cast many a surreptitious glance over his shoulder.

He should have taken time to hunt for, and kill the devil horse, then he would feel certain that all was well, but the superstitious urge to leave that place at once had been overpowering.

As he left the coulée of death further and further behind, his confidence grew. He'd cross Cherry Creek and skirt the badlands, making for the small but lawless town of Peaceful, which he believed was somewhere near Hot Springs in Wyoming.

From there he could make his way down through Colorado and eventually lose himself in Mexico. Once he'd crossed the Rio Grande no one would ever find him. He would buy a huge hacienda and live in luxury for the rest of his life on the money in the burlap sacks.

The thoughts were good, Sanchos told himself. A

buzzard wheeled overhead and the Mexican gave an involuntary shudder as he pushed his plodding horse into a canter.

He'd noon at Cherry Creek he decided, but then push right on as fast as he could.

Sanchos was eager to shake the dust of the South Dakotas from his mount's hooves as quickly as possible.

'The wolf is dead yet still I run like the jackal,' he muttered.

SEVEN

As Eli Kyle made his way across the South Dakotas he began to feel the excitement of 'coming home'. He would soon be travelling the lands of the Pawnee, the place where his father had taken a squaw. The results of that union had been himself.

Although he could remember very little of that early life he seemed to recall the love and care he had received until his father had raped the Pawnee chief's wife.

He could vaguely remember being snatched up by his father in the dead of night. A wild kaleidoscope ride through darkness with the scream of irate men behind them.

He knew that the Pawnee people would not condemn him for his father's sins, and one day he hoped to return to these lands to be with them.

Eli knew that he would never be accepted by the whites no more than he had been accepted by his father's second wife, that slim, weak thing who had been the mother of Nathaniel.

Hate surged in him as he thought of Nathaniel, the man who had broken Eli's one anchor of friendship, the nearest thing he had ever known to love in a hostile world.

A Wolf and a Jackal

He had lost it all, that day his half-brother had killed their father.

Then, before Eli could take his revenge, Nathan had run like the coward he was.

Nathaniel! The fair-haired, blue-eyed favourite of his mother. A man Eli had sneered at and dominated because not only was he the eldest, but he was also jealous of the love Nathan's white mother showered upon her son.

With his father's tacit agreement, he had punished Nathan unmercifully until that fateful day when his half-brother realized that he had at last outgrown Eli and had been able to return the injustices in full measure.

That was when Eli had started practising with a gun, an old, worn-out Colt Patterson of his father's.

It was no longer usable as a gun but Eli practised drawing it from a side holster for hours on end. One day soon all that practice would pay off: Nathaniel would lie dead at his feet and Eli would have achieved his goal.

He dismounted and stripped off his black suit, boots and hat. His underclothes quickly followed and he stood there, naked, before donning a breech clout, moccasins and a sweat band from his pack.

Eli felt free at last; when in Indian country live like an Indian. That had been his father's maxim and it worked.

Only the pack mule showed his white breeding. No Indian would ever need it.

Nathan's wagon had been standing beside Cherry Creek for three full days.

The water was clear, sweet and fast running. The fishing was good and it made a nice change from horse meat.

The young man in the wagon had sweated through a

fever for twenty-four hours, and at one time in the night Nathan was sure the boy had passed over. But then, quite suddenly, he started to breathe easily again, and the worst was past.

Yesterday Sarah could tell Nathan that the young man's name was Jeff Mason, and from the few words he had managed, she had discovered that he had been responsible for the two dead bodies in the coulée.

Nathan could not understand how the young man had managed to stay conscious long enough to point and fire his gun so accurately at the killer lying in wait for them. Still less could he understand how one so young could account for the killing of two seasoned outlaws with such fearsome reputations.

The fish was ready and Nathan took some to the end of the wagon so that Sarah could try to feed it to the lad, who seemed much brighter today.

'Think you could take some of this fish, son?' he asked solicitously.

'I think I could eat a horse, saddle and all, sir,' croaked Jeff with a weak grin. 'Just don't ask me to ride it first.'

'Well now,' grinned Nathan. 'Seems the lad's got a sense of humour, Sarah. Are you up to talking, lad? or should we just eat this fish before it gets cold?'

Nathan was startled by the snuffle of a horse behind him.

He turned in quick consternation to find six Indians sitting their ponies within a few yards of him.

They stared at Nathan without a word, evidently making up their minds whether to launch an attack or not, depending on how many others were in the wagon.

So far there had been no great trouble with the Indians, but they were getting increasingly restive at the number of white men crossing their lands, mostly to go to more settled parts. So, anyone deciding to cross, what was generally known as 'Indian territory' was taking a grave risk.

Nathan mentally cursed himself for his laxity. These men should never have been able to get so close without him knowing.

There was an uneasy stir among the Indians as Sarah eased back the tarp with the muzzle of the shot-gun.

They knew of these things and had seen the damage such a thing could do.

One of the Indians, obviously the leader of the group, raised his hand in the sign of peace and gabbled something in his own language.

'He's asking why you are invading his hunting grounds,' husked Jeff.

'You understand snake's tongue?' asked Nathan in surprise.

'Put the gun down, ma'am,' said Jeff quietly. 'And would you please pull the tarp right back so that we can see each other, sir?'

Nathan, after some hesitation, slowly drew back the tarp.

'I offer greetings to the *Otceti Cacowin Tetons*,' Jeff said hoarsely in perfect Siouan.

'You speak our tongue!' replied the leader in quick surprise.

'It is an honour to do so. How are you called?'

'I am called Bear Claw; how is it you speak our tongue?'

'You know of Eagle Eye of the Hunkapapas and his sons?'

'I know of these. They are our brothers of the seven council fires for we are of the Oglalas.'

'I am the adopted son of Eagle Eye and brother to Swift Arrow. I am called Broken Feather; it was all I could find in my warrior test,' Jeff tried to shrug and gave a lopsided grin while the Indians whooped and hooted with laughter, all except Bear Claw.

'You are a long way from the Hunkapapas' hunting grounds. Is Eagle Eye well?'

Jeff shook his head. 'I am here because the men who killed Eagle Eye and his son, together with my true mother and father have passed this way. I have killed many along the road of vengeance, but there is one other, so I must continue. Will you permit us to cross your hunting grounds?'

'We will help you in your vengeance if you wish it.'

'The vengeance is mine, and no man shall deny me the right.' Jeff's voice shook with suppressed emotion.

Bear Claw raised his hand. 'Go in peace, and return when you wish. Call and we will be there. May *Kitchi Manito* guide your arm while the spirit of Eagle Eye watches over you. How are you called by your people?'

'I am called Mason.'

'We are proud to have known you, Mason.'

'And I you, Bear Claw.'

The six wheeled away as one and galloped off without a backward glance.

'Wow!' gasped Sarah. 'What was all *that* about?'

Jeff lay back exhausted. 'You reckon I've earned that piece of fish, ma'am? My stomach is grumbling worse than a sister-in-law at a funeral, as Mother used to say.'

Sarah picked up the tin plate and began to spoonfeed the fish into his mouth while Nathan reached forward to pick up the shot-gun.

Jeff raised his hand. 'You won't need that, sir; Bear Claw has given us his word. The only people we *might*

A Wolf and a Jackal

have to worry about now are the Pawnee and possibly the Cheyenne but they won't bother us while our friends are around, and believe me they won't ever be very far away.'

'D'you feel like tellin' us about it, son?' asked Nathan. 'You don't have to of course, but it might help us to understand some of the things you've had to do, like those *hombres* in the coulée for instance.'

So between mouthfuls of fish Jeff told how his parents had been murdered and how Eagle Eye and Swift Arrow had given their lives to save his.

Jeff told of his vow to the Indian chief, that he would exact vengeance from the whole gang, and how he had done so, except for one man. How he had forgiven Sanchos and how the Mexican had betrayed him for greed.

'Which was why you found me in that coulée back there. Sanchos tried to kill me; in fact he thinks he did. One day he's gonna regret he didn't make sure while he still had the chance,' Jeff concluded.

'Phew!' muttered Nathan. 'You sure make it sound easy, fella. Fifteen huh?'

'Fourteen,' corrected Jeff tersely. 'I still want that sneaky Mex.' He lay back exhausted. 'I'd be obliged if I could kind of drift along with you folks for a while,' he murmured almost shyly. 'Seems a long time since I had real friendly folk around.'

Nathan smiled at Sarah. 'Be like havin' a kid brother around. D'you think we could put up with another body in this here wagon?' he asked slyly.

'Don't worry about that, sir,' replied Jeff, mistaking the levity for a serious question. 'I'll sleep anywhere.'

'I reckon we can find room for one more, Nathaniel,' agreed Sarah.

Selfconsciously she bustled her husband out of the wagon.

'Don't be standing around now, Nathan,' she admonished. 'Young Jeff may be full but I could eat some of that fish if you'd like to put one on the griddle, and some coffee would hit the spot too. How about it, Jeff, you fancy some coffee?'

She turned quickly when Jeff did not answer, and a tender smile flitted across her face as she realized that he was already sound asleep.

Sarah climbed slowly from the wagon and walked quietly towards Nathan.

He turned questioningly, and she put her arms around him, drawing his head down to her.

'Thank you, Nathan,' she murmured, as a rebellious tear ran down her cheek. 'He's too old to be our son, but if the day ever comes I'd like ours to grow up like him.'

He drew her close, knowing he could hardly speak for the lump in his own throat so he kissed her, slowly, gently telling her without words of the way he felt, and would always feel for this tiny, determined but tempestuous woman.

EIGHT

Sanchos made three attempts to bury the money he was carrying before he finally entered the town.

Peaceful was no place to be carrying sacks of cash around, and the fact that he was a Mexican would only make matters worse. He knew that the white people here were no better than animals.

Most, if not all of them were running from something and he could expect to be kicked and pushed around as a matter of course. To these people Mexicans were on a par with the Indians and halfbreeds, to be treated as beneath contempt, the butt of any white man's anger.

Each time Sanchos attempted to either bury the money, or secrete it under a pile of rocks, he would look up and see a scavenger in the sky. To his superstitious mind it was a spy watching him for the man he called *El Lobo*. Then Sanchos would stop what he was doing and scurry away to hide until the thing had gone.

'I am indeed a jackal,' he muttered in self-contempt when he had at last managed to hide his money. 'But I *shall* realize my dream of a hacienda and great respect. Once I get to Mexico I shall be a *jefe* so I will stay but a few days in this heathen town to buy supplies and then move on.'

The town was like an anthill as men rode into and out

of the small ramshackle town. The cheap timber-framed structures were already twisting and bowing in the intense heat.

Sanchos rode slowly down the centre of the dirt road, his serape pulled around himself effectively hiding his holstered sixgun and sheathed machete. His sombrero was tilted forward shielding his face, giving the impression of tired indolence. But his eyes were needle sharp, absorbing everything around him as his horse plodded slowly on.

He passed three saloons, almost one beside the other. The batwings never stopped swinging so trade was obviously brisk.

Sanchos breathed a sigh of relief as he reached the end of the dirt road and things began to quieten down.

He was relieved to see a *cantina*. At least it meant that there were other Mexicans in this God-forsaken hole, and he could get a few nights' lodging without having to try one of the two clapped-out hotels he'd passed.

Hotels meant white men, and they meant trouble.

He slid from the saddle and wandered into the cool interior.

Sanchos could never quite understand why gringos built their buildings of timber when adobe was so much cooler, and with a little attention lasted far longer.

Tilted sombreros told of men taking a siesta in the cool gloom.

Even the *patron* behind the bar was nodding in an armchair tilted back against the wall.

The chair tipped forward on to its four legs as Sanchos tapped the counter with a silver dollar.

'*Tequila* patron, por favor,' grunted Sanchos.

The man was very fat with a wide, almost flat face. Greasy hair hung in lank strands from under his

A Wolf and a Jackal

sombrero, joining forces with his long moustachios.

He placed the bottle on the counter beside a dish of salt, whipped up the dollar and slapped the change on the bar without a word, almost as if he begrudged being disturbed even by a customer.

'You have a room perhaps, *señor?*' queried Sanchos politely.

'A room!' The man positively beamed; his fat round face spread even more as he pulled at his long moustachios. '*Si, señor*, we have the very best rooms. For ten *centavos* a night you can be favoured with the best room of all. You have the luggage?' he queried suspiciously.

'No luggage,' replied Sanchos sadly. 'Just dollars.'

He placed a second silver dollar on the table, which was quickly whisked away.

'Then who needs the luggage? Please to follow me *señor*,' grinned the *patron*.

Sanchos picked up his bottle and the dish of salt.

'I have travelled many miles, *señor*,' he said, as he followed the *patron* up the stairs. 'So I do not wish to be disturbed. Tomorrow I shall want a bath and plenty of food. I do not expect any change from the dollar you have, and tomorrow I will give you another.'

The *patron* almost broke his neck attempting to bow and turn while still climbing the stairs. 'Your slightest wish, *señor*, is my pleasure,' he assured, wondering exactly how many more dollars the man had to spend.

His interest quickly waned, however, when they entered the room, and Sanchos removed his serape to reveal the tied-down holster on one side and the machete on the other.

Sanchos was well aware of the man's thoughts. He grinned slyly. 'Forgive me, *señor*, but I am of very nervous disposition so please ensure my complete privacy.'

The machete flicked from his waist and thumped into the doorframe. 'It would be a great pity if some innocent soul should be skewered – by accident you understand.'

The patron's colour drifted three shades lighter as Sanchos removed the machete from the frame with obvious difficulty.

'*Señor*, I can assure you complete privacy no matter how long you sleep,' the barman stuttered as he backed towards the door and pulled it closed behind him.

It was four days later when Nathan settled on a camp-site on the banks of a small river some six miles out of town and paid a visit to the sorry jumble of warped and twisted clapboard buildings known as Peaceful.

He'd decided to ride the palomino to give it some exercise.

Nathan bought some groceries and eggs at the dry goods store, some ammunition to replenish his depleted stock and a few small luxuries for Sarah.

He did not want to be away too long because Jeff had received a bit of a setback with his head wound, and while he felt sure that at a pinch Sarah and Jeff could manage, he'd be happier once he had the wagon in sight again.

Sanchos was standing outside the *cantina* smoking a thin Mexican cheroot and enjoying the feeling of a good midday meal inside him as Nathan rode by.

He stiffened at the sight of the palomino.

It was impossible! It could not be the same one! *But it was*! Sanchos knew it.

There was a bitter taste in his mouth and he realized

A Wolf and a Jackal

that he had bitten his cheroot in two.

He spat it out as he tried to bring reason to his chaotic thoughts.

He should be pleased, he told himself; this *hombre* must have found the horse wandering around. Which must mean that the man he was so afraid of was dead.

But *was* he! Sanchos asked himself, and why would the horse be here of all places?

Sanchos felt a coldness along his spine as his superstitions began to take hold.

'First the scavengers in the sky,' he muttered. 'Now I see his horse. What does this mean?'

His horse was tied at the hitch rail so he decided to follow the man. 'I might even try to buy it from the gringo,' he muttered. 'Then I could shoot it and it would be gone forever.'

As they rode out of town, places of concealment lessened and he found himself having to leave more and more space between himself and his quarry.

Sanchos was taking shelter behind some large rocks a few miles from town when Bear Claw and two braves seemed to appear from nowhere in the heat-haze ahead.

They were riding at a pace that rapidly overhauled the man in front of them.

Sanchos smiled as the Indians closed with the rider. Perhaps he wouldn't have to shoot the horse after all.

The smile changed to a frown as the man greeted the Indians as if they were friends.

A cold knot of fear settled in his stomach as he began to understand by the hand signals that they were telling the man he was being followed.

Quite suddenly the Indians turned their mounts and began to ride rapidly towards his hiding-place, emitting a series of yips and shouts.

Sanchos turned his own mount; keeping the line of rocks between himself and the Indians he raced for the safety of the town. Sanchos knew the Indians would not even think of entering the white man's town.

Sanchos had planned to leave in the next day or so, but now he realized that he could not leave without making sure the man he feared was truly dead or not, and if he was not dead then he, Sanchos, would have to pay someone to kill him. 'That's if he *can* be killed,' he muttered despondently.

Sanchos was tying his horse to the hitch rail when he saw the man in black riding down the centre of the street.

Sanchos, like many other outlaws, had heard of this man. Eli Kyle, a halfbreed bounty hunter, a man feared by the most hardened of outlaws.

If his enemy was indeed alive this was the man who could deal with him. It would cost good money but Sanchos was prepared to pay well to be rid of Jeff Mason.

Sanchos walked away, covertly watching the halfbreed as he tied his horse to the rail next to his own mount.

The Mexican quarter was the only place a halfbreed could get a drink or a room without causing considerable upset so there would be plenty of chances for Sanchos to strike up a conversation with the man if he needed to.

NINE

Nathan was worried about the unknown rider the Indians had seen following him. He had taken some time over the identification of the man.

He wished he could speak the language, but in the end Nathan had managed to understand that the follower was Mexican, so he could be relieved that his brother had not yet caught up with them.

Nathan looked into the wagon as he tied the palomino to the tailgate.

'How is he, Sarah?' he asked.

'Not good,' she replied. 'In fact I believe the fever's getting worse rather than better. It's possible that the bullet bouncing off his skull might have caused some internal injury. The wound is certainly infected and we might have to lance it if it doesn't break soon.'

Jeff was unconscious; his breathing was heavy and the sweat was running down a face that was pale and drawn making him look considerably older than he was.

'He sure don't look up to travelling,' agreed Nathan. 'There was a man following me today. Bear Claw and a couple of his braves chased him off.'

'Not Eli?' asked Sarah in quick alarm.

Nathan shook his head. 'From what I could understand it was a Mex. I was wonderin' if it might not be the same *hombre* who tried to close young Jeff's book, so I'll sleep under the wagon tonight just in case we get snoopers.'

'You know you can't sleep peaceful under there, Nathaniel,' protested Sarah. 'Those dreams always come when you sleep under the wagon.'

'It's time I faced up to 'em anyway, Sarah. They've haunted me for too long.'

Nathan collected his blanket and laid it out between the wheels. He placed the shot-gun on the edge of it, turning the blanket over the gun to protect it from the sandy soil.

Nathan kissed Sarah. 'Get some rest, gal,' he muttered. 'Let's hope he's through the worst of it by morning. Call me if you need me.'

'Try to get a good night yourself, Nathan,' replied Sarah, 'Shall we take turn about?'

'I don't think so, hon; that palomino of Jeff's will kick up hell if anyone comes a'calling. Goodnight.'

Nathan crawled under the wagon and lay staring up at the floor of it just above his head. It was true, each time he slept under the wagon he dreamed of his past, and even now his mind cringed from what he knew was about to happen.

He allowed himself to relax, breathing deeply and evenly, but inevitably his mind began its backward track – back to his younger days—

Nathaniel lay on his cot listening to his mother's quiet, sobbing cries.

He heard the sharp cracking sound of a slap, his mother's whimpering scream and his father's voice telling her to shut her stupid mouth as he hit her yet again.

Nathan was seventeen now and he had been listening to his father beat his mother more and more over the years.

It was getting so that he could not sleep without hearing his mother's voice in his dreams.

Eli would sit in the other cot chuckling as he listened to his father beating the white woman. He would jeer at Nathan for covering his ears.

'He's gonna give her what for in a minute Nate,' he'd say. 'That old bed will be a-groanin' away like hell in a minute.'

And that was just the way it would be. Eli grunted in time with the noise.

Nathan buried his head under the clothes so that he could not hear the noises from the other bedroom, but he could not help hearing Eli, gasping and groaning.

Nathan was glad when he heard Eli give that final gasping moan. He knew that Eli would go to sleep now and leave him be.

But this night it was different.

He heard his mother give a gut-wrenching scream followed by a howl of laughter from his father.

'Don't like yer hair pulled, eh?' he laughed, as he slapped her. 'This is a special night, you white trash.' He laughed again as he slapped her once more.

'Eli's of age now; it's time he was broke in.'

'What d'you mean, Matthew?' he heard his mother ask through her sobs.

'What the hell do you think I mean woman!' he shouted. 'It's time Eli became a man; he's gone twenty summers an' he ain't never had a woman yet.'

'Oh no-o Matthew. Not that! *Please!*'

The plea ended with a cry as he slapped her twice, very hard.

'Why not, fer God's sake,' he snarled. 'The kid's got to find hisself an' there's no other woman around is there?'

'But, he's like a son to me, Matthew. I brought him up! He's kin for God's sake.'

'Don't talk like a stupid cow, 'course he ain't kin, well, not yours anyway so it don't make no difference. It's time he was broke in an' yore gonna do it.'

'No Matthew! I won't do it and you can't make me!'

There was a loud scream. 'Don't like that do yuh?' he laughed. 'You'll do as I say and like it my girl.'

Nathan winced as he heard his mother scream again.

Nathan realized that Eli had stopped his grunting and gasping some little while ago, and now he was sitting up staring at the door expectantly.

'Eli, get in here right now!' yelled his father, 'an' don't bother with yer pants, that's one thing you *won't* need.'

Eli leapt off the bed; he was stark naked. 'Comin' Paw,' he shouted, excitement pitching his voice high.

He turned to Nathan. 'You hear that, little brother?' he crowed excitedly. 'It's my time now. *Yahoo!*'

Nathan tried not to listen, but even with his head buried under the clothes and his fingers in his ears, he could still hear his father and Eli grunting and groaning, while his mother cried.

Then there was a long silence and the whole thing would start all over again.

The next night Eli told him he could have the bedroom for himself.

'I'm sleepin' with Paw from now on,' he told Nathan, with a superior grin. 'Me one side, Paw t'other, an yore ma in the middle. You can bet that twixt the two of us she ain't gonna get much time tuh sleep.'

Matthew and Eli grabbed his mother's arms, pushed her into the bedroom and closed the door.

A Wolf and a Jackal

'Git to your room, Nathan,' growled his father. 'Your turn will come in a year or so.'

They were about to follow his mother into the room when there was a shot, followed by the noise of someone falling.

All three rushed into the room.

Nathan could see his mother stretched out on the floor.

The top half of her head was splattered all over the bed and Matthew's gun lay on the floor beside her.

She'd obviously put the gun in her mouth and pulled the trigger and the results were horrific.

Eli started to vomit, while Matthew began cursing.

That was when Nathan walked slowly out of the room. There was a dreamlike air about him; everything seemed to be happening in slow motion as he lifted his father's Sharps single-shot, hunting musket from its hook over the front door.

He pulled back the hammer and waited until his father walked out of the bedroom, still cursing.

The look of sheer horror on his father's face was like nectar to Nathan.

'No, no. I'm your father, Nathan,' he shouted desperately, as he started to charge across the room.

Even that mad charge seemed slow and it gave Nathan ample time to see his father's eyes widen even further as he realized what was about to happen.

Nathan pulled the trigger, watching in a kind of unreal fascination as his father's face slowly disintegrated before his eyes.

He heard an anguished, animal scream as Eli entered the room and saw the carnage wrought by the big .50 calibre ball.

There was vomit dripping from his chin and his eyes

were wild with hate as he stood in total shock, staring from his father to Nathan.

'You've killed him!' he screeched. 'You dirty, no good sonofabich, you've killed my paw!'

He paused, pointing a trembling finger at Nathan as he backed into the bedroom. 'I'll kill you Nathan,' he muttered savagely. 'You're gonna die.'

Eli turned, moving swiftly into the bedroom, and Nathan realized that Eli was going to get the pistol his mother had used to kill herself.

He threw the now useless musket at the bedroom door in blind panic as everything began to speed up once more.

Then he began to run – out of the house and across the yard towards the barns. Anywhere to get away from Eli's wrath.

He heard the boom of his father's old Dragoon Colt behind him and it lent wings to his flying feet.

A second and third boom followed.

He heard a ball smash into the timber barn beside him as Eli fired again and again.

Nathan was whimpering incoherently as he threw saddle and bridle on to one of the horses. He was about to mount when he realized that Eli would catch him unless he did something to slow him down.

He heard Eli's curses fading as he opened the stalls and herded the restless horses into the centre aisle, then he cautiously opened the main barn door.

It was quiet out there and Nathan reasoned that Eli had returned to the house to get some more ammunition for the pistol before continuing to hunt him down.

He pushed his way back through the horses, picked up a bull whip and mounted the horse he'd saddled.

A Wolf and a Jackal

Fear was bile in Nathan's mouth as he cracked the whip and shouted at the top of his voice to stampede the horses, driving his own mount amongst them to cause even more panic.

As they crossed the yard Nathan saw Eli's form silhouetted against the open door of the house. Eli was screaming like a maniac, almost drowning the heavy boom of the Colt.

'I'll get you, Nathan,' he screeched. 'I'll find you if it takes forever. You'll always be lookin' over your shoulder, an' I'll always be there.'

The gun banged again as Nathan clung to the racing horse and cried bitter tears.

Nathaniel suddenly came awake under the touch of his wife's hand, the tears still in his eyes.

'Again Nathan?' she asked quietly.

'Yeah,' he muttered. 'But I'm gettin' there, honey.'

He realized it was still full dark and pulled Sarah down to him.

'How long to sun-up?' he asked.

'You ain't bin asleep above an hour,' she replied, knowing he wanted the night to be over.

'You go back to the wagon now,' he murmured.

'Not this time,' she replied firmly. 'There's nothing more I can do for Jeff now. It'll just have to burst in its own good time so I'm sleepin' where I belong for the rest of the night.' She snuggled into the crook of his arm.

'We'll fight this thing together, Nathaniel, the way God meant us to.'

'You're right welcome, ma'am,' he replied with a lightness he was far from feeling as he pulled her closer.

In moments he was asleep.

Sarah lay awake for hours pondering over the life Eli's hate had made them lead.

One day she hoped it would all be over, and they could lead a normal life. Live in a real house like regular folks, and who knows, maybe even have children. It wasn't too late even now.

A small wistful smile pulled at her lips in the darkness. It could all be so different if there was no Eli, no nemesis of impending doom to blight their lives.

She'd even found herself praying that one of the outlaws Eli sometimes chased for their bounty would prove too good for Eli's gun and that he would be killed, only to admonish herself afterwards for asking God to perform such a wicked deed.

Slowly her eyes closed and she fell into a fitful sleep.

TEN

Sanchos left the doubtful comfort of his room once the day's brightness began to fade and rode slowly out of town towards the rocks he had left so recently.

He allowed his horse to plod steadily past the rocks, knowing that as soon as one horse scented the other on the night air they would whicker a greeting and that would guide him to the camp.

About half an hour later he heard the snuffling of horses ahead.

Sanchos slid quickly from the saddle and put his hand over his own mount's muzzle to prevent it from whickering.

He waited for a long time, testing the light breeze for sounds of movement, watching the silhouette of his horse against a skyline which gradually lightened as the moon's light reflected over the horizon. His horse was staring directly forward with its ears cocked, listening to the other horses.

Sanchos was satisfied. He slowly led his mount forward until he could see the darker patches of three horses. A little beyond that he could see the darker shape of a wagon.

One of the horses gave another whicker and began to approach and, as the light strengthened, he recognized the palomino.

Sanchos stood perfectly still but the horse had recognized his scent. It did not fear this man so it came ambling over.

The Mexican slowly drew his knife.

He could slit its throat and be gone as silently as he had arrived.

The horse pushed its head into the man's chest as if waiting for a greeting and Sanchos patted its head with one hand while he slowly raised the knife to the animal's jugular.

Jeff was sweating profusely and his head was banging away like a drum.

His forehead was swelling rapidly and he was hallucinating badly.

He realized he was alone. The moon was shining directly into the rear of the wagon where the tarp was not fully pulled across.

Jeff heard his horse whicker but it was not alarmed, more the greeting of a friend, or had he imagined it he wondered.

He had to move. His head felt as if it was about to burst, the claustrophobic effect of the wagon seemed to be crushing him. The open section at the rear was drawing Jeff like a magnet and he slowly began to drag himself towards it.

Sanchos paused with the knife against the palomino's neck as he heard the wagon groan softly from movement within.

He sheathed the knife and drew his gun.

Whoever was in the wagon would have to die. He would whip back the tarp and fire into the wagon, he decided. The cayuse could die later.

Jeff's head was pounding faster and faster. He had to

A Wolf and a Jackal

get to the opening.

Sanchos snatched back the tarp as his gun came up.

He found himself staring into the dreaded face of El Lobo!

Unknown to Jeff the swelling had burst. Blood and pus was pouring down his face.

To Sanchos, Jeff looked exactly as he had that day in the coulée! Dead, with blood pouring down a face made yellow by the brightness of the moon.

Only he was still alive!

All the superstitions of his race together with his own beliefs of El Lobo Diablo were confirmed in that fleeting moment.

Sanchos screamed then, a womanish, high-pitched scream. He forgot he was holding a gun. Sanchos forgot everything except the awful need to get away from this place as fast as possible.

The gun fell from nerveless fingers and he ran.

Faster than he ever thought possible.

Sanchos literally threw himself into his saddle.

He did not hear Nathan's shout nor the bang of the shot-gun. Sanchos leaned as far forward in the saddle as he possibly could. Gouging his horse with wildly flailing spurs, he called upon long forgotten saints to save him from the thing in the wagon, a thing that could bleed forever yet never die.

Sanchos rode into town at a mad gallop. He threw himself from his horse, charged up the outside staircase to his room and collapsed across the bed.

He squeezed his eyes shut against the awful sight of that face staring at him with all that blood and muck over it.

It was impossible, but he'd seen it with his own eyes. The man he had named El Lobo was somehow still alive.

Sanchos rolled off the bed, grabbed the almost full bottle of tequila from the rickety dresser and took a large swallow.

A second and a third followed. The terror began to fade. His shaking hands began to settle and the acrid knot in his belly began to ease.

Sanchos was sure of one thing: never again would he attempt to go against this devil. He would pay others to do the job for him, and meanwhile he would run.

Hiding wherever he could he would lose himself over the Rio Grande where he could use his money to buy as many men as he needed to do his bidding, men who would kill their own mothers for a few pesos.

'This Eli Kyle,' he muttered. 'He seems afraid of no one, and he has killed many. I will offer him one thousand pesos for this man's head, cut from his body and delivered to me in person so that I might stick it on a pole as food for the vultures.'

ELEVEN

The first inclination Nathan had that something was wrong was the high-pitched scream.

He reached for the shot-gun but was impeded by Sarah, who was lying on his arm with part of her body over the gun.

The delay allowed the intruder to get to his horse and Nathan could see him swinging aboard.

He fired in reflex, realizing that he had very little chance of a hit over the distance.

He fired the second barrel just in case there was more than one man in the raid, but after the quick flurry of galloping hooves the silence of the night returned, except for a sobbing, gasping sound coming from the rear of the wagon.

Nathan hurried towards the noise but Sarah was there first.

'Quick Nathan give me a hand,' Sarah called sharply.

Nathan stopped, shocked by the blood-and-pus-covered face staring from the back of the wagon.

'What the he—' Nathan began.

'Never mind the blasphemy,' interrupted Sarah tartly. 'The infection's burst. Help me get him out of the wagon so that I can cleanse the wound.'

They lifted him down together and Nathan dragged

the blanket from under the wagon to use as makeshift pillow, while Sarah climbed into the wagon and returned ripping a shirt to pieces.

'Build up the fire, Nathan, we'll need some hot water to bathe the poor man's head. We should know in a few hours if he's going to win or lose this particular fight.'

They worked over him together for hours, laying hot poultices over the wound, talking to him, calming Jeff as he hallucinated about his dead mother and father, holding his hands as he fought those other battles over again.

Then came the tears, the great sobbing tears that told Sarah of a grief held at bay for so long, being gradually released.

It started with just a few teardrops trickling down the young man's face, but quickly built into gut-wrenching sobs that threatened to tear him apart. It told of the utter desolation and deep loneliness of a very young man plunged into the depths of despair.

But it also brought calmness, a release from the inner constraints his will had imposed upon him so that he could avenge his family. Finally he slept.

Sarah slowly released Jeff's hand and with a slight groan struggled to her feet.

Nathan was there to help her; she'd been kneeling in the same position for over three hours and her legs were a mass of aches from cramp.

She smiled tiredly at Nathan as she took his hand and squeezed it gently.

'D'you think he's gonna make it, lass?'

Sarah nodded, her heart was too full to speak. She'd helped Jeff fight every step of the way and now she was exhausted.

'How about a nice cup of coffee, honey?' asked

Nathan, deeply concerned at the utter exhaustion her face reflected.

Sarah nodded her thanks as she slowly made her way to the wagon. She almost crawled over the tailgate and flopped on to the bed. She was fast asleep long before Nathan had made the coffee.

Nathan stared over the tailgate at his sleeping wife, sipping the coffee he had made for her.

He told himself for the thousandth time that he must do something about Eli so that they could settle down in a real home somewhere. Sarah deserved better than trailing around in a wagon year after year, always watching their back trail, hoping against hope that Eli would eventually give up, yet knowing he never would.

Nathan made his decision that day as he looked at his sleeping wife.

It was time to face Eli. He'd hidden behind a preacher's collar for too long. As soon as Jeff was fit enough to be moved they'd take the wagon close to town and join the collection of wagons camped near the Mexican quarter.

The wagoners were preparing for the trek into the place known as Wyoming. Once there was sufficient people to create a wagon train big enough to give protection from the warlike Cheyenne and Shoshone, they'd blaze a new trail into virtually unknown territory and build a real home at last.

The wagon train was almost ready, and with any luck he could travel with them. If Eli caught up with them he'd face him and take his chances.

The decision made, Nathan felt a kind of release. What happened from now on was in the lap of the gods.

Nathan threw the dregs of the coffee into the fire and began to collect up their gear. He checked on Jeff as he continued with the chores. The young man was breathing easily now. It looked as though he was on the mend at last. Sleep was a great healer and Jeff seemed to be getting his share.

Nathan kept the shot-gun close, searching for anything even slightly suspicious as he fed and watered the horses.

The chores over, Nathan squatted beside the wagon and rolled himself a quirley.

Although his eyes were constantly scanning the area he could not help allowing his mind to wander back to that time when he had galloped away from his home with nothing but the clothes on his back and the horse he was riding. He remembered Eli screaming and shouting, calling him every filthy name he could think of. It seemed as if the memory of that ride would live with him forever.

Nathan's eyes gradually became heavy as the tranquillity of the moonlight carried him gently into sleep, the cigarette slipping from lax fingers—

Young Nathan had been riding for three days, or was it four? He couldn't rightly recall.

He had no weapons except a small knife. Twice he'd tried to catch a cottontail but without the necessary snares he knew he was wasting his time.

He dimly remembered dropping a rock on the head of a rattlesnake to kill it, but after skinning it his stomach churned at the thought of eating it raw, and he had no way of lighting a fire.

Angry at his own inability to stomach the snake he'd tossed it away. Almost before it hit the ground a vulture had dropped from the sky and swept it away.

Was that only yesterday? he wondered, as he sat his tired horse, staring at nothing.

There was some rocky ground ahead leading into a

A Wolf and a Jackal

large stand of trees that could well prove to be the beginnings of a regular forest.

Might be a good place to find something to eat, and he sure could do with some grub before his stomach just plain forgot what food was, he ruminated dejectedly.

He was startled out of his reverie by the sound of a rifle shot followed by the sound of a bullet's passing.

Nathan instinctively kicked his horse into motion and leaned over the horse's neck to present as small a target as possible as the gun cracked again.

Nathan glanced over his shoulder. Eli had been too eager.

Firing from the back of a horse was chancy at best, but with the horse moving at almost a gallop it was a wonder Nathan had even heard the passing of the first bullet.

He set his mount into a zig-zagging run towards the stand of timber as Eli tried again to pick him off with a lucky shot, but Nathan was into the first of the trees by this time and he was soon lost to sight.

His first panic over, Nathan began to ride with more care, keeping to clear ground where the hoof prints would not leave a trail, until he came to a close bunch of trees surrounded by smaller bushes. He carefully walked his horse into the tiny glade and left it ground hitched.

Nathan backed out of the bushes and checked that there was no obvious signs of his entry before carefully back-tracking, and covering any tell-tale signs he had left in passing.

Nathan knew Eli was a reasonable tracker, but he was no slouch himself, and his hunger made him want to find Eli.

His quick backward glance when the shots had been fired told Nathan that Eli had come prepared. He had been towing a loaded packhorse, and that meant food.

Nathan suddenly froze as the clink of a horseshoe sounded very close.

He almost jumped as Eli screamed at the top of his voice, 'I know you're here, Nathan, you murderin' rat, an' I'll find you if it takes the rest of my life. You hear me?'

Nathan heard Eli dismount and begin to scurry around, obviously looking for sign.

He'd find very little, Nathan thought, as he slowly back-tracked away.

Dusk was beginning to creep in and Nathan guessed that Eli would not move much further before morning. Meanwhile he would try to find some berries to help ease his hunger pains, until it became dark enough to try to steal some of Eli's provisions.

It was full dark as Nathan cautiously crept towards Eli's camp. The stale smell of bacon was ambrosia to Nathan's taste buds and he was having difficulty in controlling his saliva as he crouched in the bushes beside the still camp.

Eli was wrapped in a blanket beside the dying fire and a sudden crack of a piece of burning wood did not even make him stir.

Nathan crept cautiously around the camp easing his way slowly towards the bulging saddle-bags.

He almost fell over a large log. He picked it up and hefted it in his hands. It would make a good club. He could kill Eli with it, he thought. One good hefty stroke and Eli would be gone forever.

Nathan shook his head in silent answer to his thoughts. He knew he couldn't kill his own brother like that.

Nathan lay the timber carefully back on the ground and continued to make his way towards the food packs near the horses.

He slipped over the ground like a wraith and paused for a moment beside the packs.

Eli hadn't moved.

Nathan lifted the packs, making no sound as he turned towards the woods.

Eli was crouched there within a few feet of him, his face stretched in a grimace of pure hate. The old Dragoon Colt was pointed at Nathan's head as the hammer clicked back.

'Got you, you sneakin' murderin' swine,' he gloated.

Nathan felt a burning searing pain behind his eyes as he tried to struggle to his feet....

Nathan came awake gasping and struggling for breath. The morning sun was a scorching ball, reflecting its heat directly into his eyes from a tin plate made shiny by years of scouring with sand.

'D'you figure you're gonna outrun him?'

Nathan switched his eyes towards the sound of the voice. Jeff was awake; their eyes met, but Nathan was the first to look away.

'Is that supposed to mean something?' he asked evasively.

'No, sir,' replied Jeff evenly. 'But seems to me you got a burr under your saddle an' you can't shift it no-how. Now, I know it ain't none of my business but ...'

'You're right, it *ain't* none of your God-damned business,' replied Nathan brusquely. 'What can you know about it anyway?'

'Like you just said, it ain't none of my business, and I don't mean no disrespect, sir, but my pa always used to say, "If there's a burr under the saddle get shut of it. The longer it stays, the bigger the hurt", an' I know just what a burr feels like, I still got one under my saddle also. It's a Mex, name of Sanchos, an' I surely do intend to do somethin' about him as soon as I'm able.'

'Did you *really* take care of the Kincaid gang on your own like you told us?' asked Nathan in curious disbelief.

'Nope.'

'No? But you told us ...'

'There's still Sanchos,' interrupted Jeff quietly. 'Was kinda mistaken about him there for a while, but....'

'Leave two men together and they'll spend the time shooting the breeze instead of making some breakfast,' scolded Sarah as she poked her head around the wagon tarp.

She peered at Jeff with her head on one side like a cheeky bird inspecting a worm.

'Well, now, young fellow-me-lad, you look a lot more chipper this morning. Bet you'd feel a darned sight better if some lazy feller got off his fat butt and cooked some breakfast,' she ended waspishly, with a sly glance at Nathan. 'I know *I* would.'

'Don't ever git married, son,' grinned Nathan as he began to kick the dying embers together. 'All women are slave-drivers.'

Sarah climbed down from the wagon with no signs of the exhaustion she had shown when she had climbed into it. Nathan was always surprised at the tiny woman's resilience.

She squatted beside Jeff as bright and cheerful as ever.

'My but he's looking a sight better today eh, Nathan?' she smiled. 'For a while there it was touch and go, but good nursing, not to mention some good *feeding*,' she jibed, glancing at Nathan, 'does the world of good.'

'All right, ma'am, *yes* ma'am,' grunted Nathan, falling into the jocular mood as the bacon began to sizzle in the pan. 'Coffee, *ma'am?*'

'That should hit the spot,' agreed Sarah, ignoring the

A Wolf and a Jackal   79

levity as she began to gently probe Jeff's wound. 'Swelling's gone down a treat; guess you'll soon be as near normal as a man ever gets.'

'For which I'd surely like to thank you both,' replied Jeff earnestly.

'D'you remember anything about last night?' asked Sarah casually.

'Some,' replied Jeff. 'Thanks for bearing with me. Seems I had a lot of grief to get rid of an' you were the only one around.'

Sarah put a protective arm around him. 'Hush now,' she murmured. 'No man should have to take what you've been through, but I was proud you let me share it.'

'You sure sound like my ma used to,' he said soberly. Then a quick boyish grin spread across his face. ''Cept she was some bigger than you and was more likely to cuff my ear than cuddle me like a yearling.'

'Reckon you could move around enough to get your back against the wagon wheel?' she asked, more to break the melancholy train of thought than to test his strength. 'That breakfast is about done if my nose is anything to go by.'

'Yes, ma'am,' replied Jeff eagerly. 'My mouth's watering somethin' awful right now.'

He slid around on his backside until his back was against the wheel while Sarah fussed around packing the blanket behind his shoulders and head.

Nathan finished cutting some large slices of bread, slid the bacon and eggs on to some tin plates and carried them across to Jeff and Sarah. Three steaming mugs of coffee followed, and in no time they were all enjoying their breakfast.

'Do I seem to remember somethin' about an intruder last night?' asked Jeff around a mouthful of bacon.

'Yeah we had visitors,' answered Nathan. 'Didn't stay long though. The state you were in, staring out of the wagon like that must have scared the shi—'

'*Nathaniel!*' Sarah cut in quickly.

'Yeah well, um, must have given him quite a scare, eh, Sarah?' Nathan amended.

'I think you were right the first time,' Sarah chuckled, as she placed her plate on the two already waiting to be washed. 'But it ain't nice to say things like that in mixed company, although I think it would be safe to say that a decent bloodhound would have no difficulty in following the smell *he* left behind.'

'Any idea who it was?' asked Jeff.

'Didn't stick around long enough to be introduced,' replied Nathan soberly. 'But I got a glimpse of his headgear. He was wearing a sombrero.'

'Sanchos!' muttered Jeff. 'I had a feeling he was still around somewhere close.'

His body had tensed at the mention of a sombrero and Sarah could see the knuckles of Jeff's hands whiten as he gripped the coffee mug.

'Easy now, son,' she soothed. 'You don't know that, it could be anybody and anyway you're in no fit state to be taking on anything bigger than a two year old just now.'

'Yeah it would make sense to get fit first,' cautioned Nathan. 'You'll only get one chance at him, son, and you can only lose once too; it would pay to remember that. Judging by the state you were in when we found you, that Mex had every right to think you were dead. It's no wonder the sight of you gave him the shock of his life. Give yourself time, don't rush it.'

'Don't worry about me, sir,' replied Jeff tersely. 'I was taught patience by an Indian chief, and the way to use a sixgun by my father. Believe me Mr Kyle there's no better teachers anywhere.'

'Oh I believe you,' grinned Nathan. 'D'you think you could drop the, mister and sir? Suppose I call you Jeff, and you call me Nathan? That sound OK to you?'

'That's fine sir – I mean Nathan,' replied Jeff, with a selfconscious grin.

'Huh,' snorted Sarah derisively, as she got to her feet.

'*Him* Nathan, *me* Sarah, and I'm the one that gets to do the dishes because that man of mine is *the* most talkative person in God's creation.'

She tapped Nathan on the head with one of the plates she'd collected. 'Come on Preacher, let's do the scouring. One invalid is quite enough, and as soon as his arm mends I'll give him some chores too, or I'll have *two* talkative men under my feet.'

Nathan stood up with a grin and a shrug at Jeff as he trailed behind his tiny wife.

The moment they had walked out of sight Jeff began to slowly ease himself upright. His arm, though stiff and sore, was not giving him any real pain, but it would be some time before he would be able to use it. Even gentle exercise was out at the moment.

As he pushed himself upright using the spokes of the wheel as leverage, Jeff felt a surge of dizziness and he almost unloaded his breakfast. Slowly the world stopped spinning and his breakfast decided to stay put. His head was thumping like a mad Indian on a war drum, but after a while that too began to ease.

Jeff held on to the spokes of the wheel for a long time before attempting to release his grip. Even then he almost fell. Another long pause, then on trembling legs he moved slowly along the side of the wagon. It seemed an impossibly long time before he eased his way around the rear of the wagon and grabbed the tailgate.

Sarah and Nathan were returning from the small stream, the dishes stacked in the large cooking pot, when Sarah spotted Jeff.

She stopped Nathan with a hand on his arm. He looked questioningly at her and she nodded in Jeff's direction.

They waited as Jeff eased himself slowly forward, placing one foot in front of the other with utter concentration.

'Did you ever see such determination?' muttered Sarah tensely.

'Did you ever look in the mirror, Sarah Kyle?' he answered succinctly.

As they watched, Jeff slowly reached into the wagon and with a great deal of effort managed to drag his Colts to him, and slip one out of its holster.

They watched spellbound as he began to make the gun gyrate through a series of intricate twists, twirls and spins. It seemed to come alive in his hand.

'An' I thought Eli was good,' muttered Nathan.

'It's a sorry day when a man who's no'but a boy should have to live with a gun in his hand,' whispered Sarah. 'A lot of men will die by that young man's hand in the years to come, you mark my words Nathaniel Kyle. It's an unholy skill he has and it will lead to an unholy end.'

Jeff seemed to sense their presence. He stopped, embarrassed, and replaced the gun before turning with a shy smile on his face as they approached.

'Sorry about that, ma'am,' he murmured. 'I didn't expect you back quite so soon. I have to practice: I can only use one hand and it ain't my best one either.'

He turned to retrace his steps. Sarah started to move forward to help him but Nathan grabbed her arm. 'Leave him be,' he muttered. 'He's testing himself. He's a

A Wolf and a Jackal 83

man who will always stand alone regardless of the odds against him.'

They watched him slowly work his way back around the wagon until he reached the wheel. Then he slowly lowered himself until he was seated once more.

That night Jeff insisted on sleeping beneath the wagon, and when Sarah protested Jeff quietly pointed out that it would be quite wrong for him to be in the wagon, fully conscious, while a man and his wife lay in the same small space.

'He has a very strict idea of what's right and wrong,' murmured Sarah to Nathan, as they lay together in the darkness.

'Brought up right,' replied Nathan.

'Mm, seems so. It surprises me that he still sees right and wrong for what it is after what he's been through.'

'God, the way he handled that gun though. It was sheer poetry,' Nathan muttered.

'Deadly poetry with only one outcome Nathaniel.'

'I sometimes wish I—'

'I don't,' interrupted Sarah, as she snuggled into her man. 'You keep wearing the collar, and we'll keep on the move. Who knows, Eli may even have lost our trail altogether by this time.'

'I guess he could have at that,' replied Nathan without conviction. 'G'night honey.'

'Goodnight Nathan, sleep well.'

Sarah was soon breathing heavily while sleep eluded Nathan, as he lay on his back staring into the darkness.

Where was Eli now? he wondered. Perhaps Sarah was right, maybe their ruse had worked and Eli had settled in with a Pawnee tribe somewhere in the Dakotas.

It was a nice thought, but in his heart Nathan knew that Jeff was right. If he wanted the burr under his saddle shifted, he'd have to do the shifting. Sooner or later Eli would demand a reckoning.

Sleep began to crowd him and he slipped back to that time in the woods, when Eli was pointing their father's Colt in his face. He'd been inches from death then....

TWELVE

The muzzle of the old Dragoon Colt looked as big as a cannon and there was nothing Nathan could do, caught as he was with the heavy pack in his hands.

'Caught you like the thieving swine you are,' Eli gloated, as he began to get up from his crouch. Spittle drooled from his mouth and Nathan fleetingly wondered if his brother was going out of his mind.

Eli seemed to tilt gradually to one side. Then it was almost as if he leaned over too far, as he crashed to the ground and lay in a heap.

'That there was one right unsociable feller, wouldn't you say?'

The voice had a deep southern drawl and came from the branch of the tree beside Eli.

The end of the branch suddenly bowed and a rather stocky young man dropped to the ground.

'Howdy pardner,' he greeted. 'That *hombre* sure had a hard head. Damn near busted my rifle barrel.' He raised the gun for closer inspection. 'Reckon I'll have to fire high and a touch to the right in future,' he chuckled as he stepped forward and thrust out a hand. 'Jason McKendrick at your service, suh,' he drawled. 'And who might I have the pleasure of addressin'?'

Nathan was still staring in wonder at the man who had

saved his life.

He was about the same age as himself but short and stocky. He wore a light-coloured stetson pushed to the back of his unruly or curly hair – in the moonlight it was hard to tell which, but even in that doubtful light he could see that both his hat and shirt were studded with conchs which glittered and flashed in the dim light.

'Name's Nathaniel. Nathaniel Kyle.'

He grabbed the proffered hand and shook it vigorously. 'An' I sure am glad you showed up when you did.'

Nathan continued to shake the hand in both of his as hard as he could in his gratitude, regardless of the other's grimace of pain.

'D'you think you-all could let me have my fingers back before you take 'em off one by one? I ain't one tuh refuse gratitude yuh understand, but let's not get carried away, there's a good feller.'

Nathan released the hand as if it were hot. 'Oh God I'm sorry Jason,' he apologised. 'I'm just so damned grateful.'

Jason blew on his fingers. 'Grateful I like. I just might need these later, if yore gratitude runs to an invite to some of that chowder for instance,' he grinned, nodding towards the heavy packs. 'I'm kinda shy on grub right now, an' hungry to boot.'

'You're right welcome, Jason. Although they really belong to him.' Nathan nodded towards Eli as he spoke.

'Oh I know *that*. I was just about to pounce myself. Shame on me, I was about to lift his dinner when you showed up with the same idea.' Jason nudged Eli with his toe.

'Any idea who the unfortuante feller is?'

'Yeah, it's my brother Eli. He was fixing to kill me.'

A Wolf and a Jackal

'Wow, brotherly love is kinda weak in your family wouldn't you say?' asked Jason, startled. 'Now just why in hell would he want to do a thing like that?'

'I killed our pa!'

'Jumpin' Jehosaphat!' ejaculated Jason, his eyes wide with shock. 'Tell me friend, how the hell do you manage about ancestors?'

'Haven't got any that I know of.'

'You *do* surprise me.' He picked up Eli's Colt and offered it to Nathan.

'D'you want to carry on your funny family tradition feller? Sounds as if it's yore turn with the gun again. Heigh ho, that's a family that was.'

Nathan threw the gun to the floor. 'It isn't like that, you don't understand,' he protested.

'Oh I *am* glad. What happened to your ma?'

'She shot herself.'

'Holy cow! And his ma?'

'Paw done for her before he ran away from a Pawnee camp after raping the chief's wife.'

'Tell me, Nathan,' asked Jason in quiet wonder. 'Does this delightful family of yours have any enemies?'

'We-ell,' replied Nathan hesitantly, 'I think the Pawnee tribe would still like to meet up with Paw.'

'I just bet they would,' whispered Jason.

Eli began to groan

'I'd think we'd best leave your brother to wake up on his own. I feel that we should be long gone before he wakes up with a sore head, don't you? Now if you'd like to bring the bags, perhaps we could find a nice quiet place to enjoy a meal and you can tell me the rest of your fascinating family history. Oh and by the way, although my given name is Jason I'm generally known as Concho.'

'I'd never have guessed,' replied Nathan with a quick

grin, as he grabbed the bags and followed his new-found friend.

When they were passing Eli's bedroll Nathan helped himself to Eli's rifle; he knew that there would be ammunition for it in the saddle-bags he was carrying.

They rode several miles, before cooking their long awaited supper.

'I reckon we should have collected your brother's hosses as well as his provisions,' Concho ruminated, as he lay picking his teeth with a sliver of wood. 'He's gonna be mad enough to eat iron and spit nails when he comes to; an' the ache in his head ain't gonna do anything to calm him down either.'

'We couldn't leave him afoot,' replied Nathan. 'The way I see it, if he's got his horse and his handgun he'll most likely go back to the ranch and forget all about it.'

'He didn't look the kind of feller to forgive and forget, more like a mix of raving lunatic and wolf, with a touch of rattler thrown in for flavouring, but you should know yore own crazy kinsfolk.' Concho threw away the sliver of wood and turned towards the dying fire. 'Oh well, it's been a long and interestin' day in its way. Guess it's me for some shut-eye,' he yawned. 'See you-all for breakfast.'

Nathan was exhausted from the trauma of the day and quickly fell into a deep sleep.

He awoke shivering in the pre-dawn chill, the clothes he wore hardly enough to warm him. He realized that he should have taken Eli's blanket while he'd had the chance, but he'd been glad to leave the camp before Eli had recovered from the blow on the head, for as Concho had said last night, Eli would be as mad as hell and would not hesitate to shoot him.

Nathan knew Eli would have actually *enjoyed* blowing

his brains all over the landscape, whereas Nathan was not at all sure that he could kill Eli. Except perhaps in a wild fit of rage.

Nathan sat up, rubbed his eyes and stared around the deserted camp.

Deserted was the word! Concho was nowhere to be seen. The horses and the pack had gone too. Nathan jumped to his feet and searched the area in the forlorn hope that Concho had merely taken the horses to some nearby stream.

It took a few seconds to sink in but Nathan soon realized that Concho had left in the night, taking the packs and horses with him, leaving Nathan afoot with just the rifle and whatever bullets were in the magazine.

Nathan was madly, screamingly angry at himself for being so trusting. But what kind of low skunk would leave a so-called friend afoot miles from anywhere?

Thinking about it, Nathan realized that Concho had shown no compunction in leaving Eli afoot. His regret was that he hadn't thought about it at the time. That should have served as a warning, but Nathan had been so pleased to have made a friend at last, that it hadn't even occurred to him.

He realized now that he had been lying with his arm over the rifle while he slept. 'Just as well,' he muttered. 'Otherwise, the thieving dog would have taken that too.'

Nathan quickly found where Concho had left the camp, and with his newly acquired rifle gripped tightly to his chest he set out to follow always acutely aware that Eli would be following on horseback with that old Dragoon Colt loaded and ready.

Nathan clutched the rifle tighter. At least, he consoled himself, he had come out that much ahead of the game.

Nathan had been plodding along through the trees

for about two hours, when he noticed that another set of tracks was overlaying those made by Concho and he quickly realized that Eli must have bypassed the camp where Nathan had been sleeping and had run across the tracks made by the thieving southerner.

Eli would already know the tracks made by Nathan's horse, and he realized that Eli must think Nathan was still ahead of him.

It was over an hour later when he heard voices raised in anger ahead.

He crept cautiously to the lip of a small basin where he could see some cowboys milling around.

His first instinct was to dash forward but then he saw that they had two prisoners.

Concho and Eli had their hands tied behind them, and were surrounded by the bunch of cowboys, whose sixguns were very much in evidence.

One heavy-set man seemed to be the leader and Nathan was so close that he could clearly hear every word.

'Where did you say you got the hoss? Just run that past me again, mister,' the man asked Concho.

'Well now, suh, as I just explained, I saw your little old ranch house in the distance an' I was about to ride right down there to see if I couldn't make a swap for my mount – with a cash adjustment of course – when, I saw this cowpoke a' riding along an—'

'Let me guess,' growled the leader sarcastically. 'He told you *he* was the owner and did the swap, took the cash as well I shouldn't wonder huh?'

'If that ain't the Lord's truth,' replied Concho piously. 'You sure do get right to the truth, mister. So with yore kind permission, I'll just be on my way.'

He started to nudge his horse forward pretending to

A Wolf and a Jackal

ignore the fact that his hands were still tied, but a series of ominous clicks brought him to an abrupt halt.

'So how about the other horses, mister? The 'breed says they belong to him.'

Concho shrugged deprecatingly. 'Sho' an' that's easy to explain, mister.'

'Do tell.'

'The 'breed sold 'em to me. Why, man, you-all know what liars *'breeds* are! He's just takin' advantage of this situation to get the horses and the saddle-bags, an' the dirty cheat is keeping my money to boot.'

'Just ain't bin your day has it?' the man replied sarcastically.

Concho turned to Eli, innocence oozing out of every pore. 'You should be downright ashamed of yourself, feller, allowing yore lowly breeding to get a-hold of you this way. You could get yourself into a whole mess of trouble with these good, upright citizens tellin' lies like that.'

Nathan watched spellbound at Concho's sheer effrontery.

Then one of the cowboys pushed his horse forward and threw a lariat over the branch of a tree.

'Hey what's that for?' asked the southerner, his voice beginning to sound less sure of himself as two men rode up and positioned themselves either side of him.

A second rope dropped over another branch, and two men rode up beside Eli.

The leader of the cowboys grinned. 'The way we figure it, mister, is that we need to find this feller who swapped one of my good broncs for that clapped-out piece of hoss-flesh you left behind. So if we haul you up there you could maybe see where he's at, and the 'breed can help yuh look. Now if you both stay up there too long you won't need these nags and we make a profit of three hosses and a pair of saddle-packs.'

The ropes were dropped over the two men's heads, and the knots were tightened under their chins.

'Now just hold on there a cotton-pickin' minute,' Concho argued, his voice taking on a pleading note. 'I can understand how you'd be keen on hanging this feller, I'd even give you-all a hand myself and be pleased to, but I'm just an honest ole cowpoke, wouldn't harm a flea. It just ain't fittin' for white folks to be hanging innocent southern gentlemen like me is it?'

His plea fell on deaf ears.

Eli sat his mount in stoic silence. He knew nothing he could say would make these men change their minds.

Nathan could hardly believe his ears. These men were about to hang two people almost without thinking about it!

'You got any last words for your Maker before we turn you into buzzard fodder?' the leader asked casually, as he turned his mount away from the men and sat slouched in the saddle, a man apart.

Even Concho had nothing more to say.

'So long fellas,' grinned the leader. 'Have a nice jig.'

The crash of a shot startled everyone in the basin.

'Let's not do anything hasty, fellas,' yelled Nathan, his voice pitched high with fear. 'You set those hosses a' running and I'll send yore boss after those two so fast he'll be waiting for 'em up yonder before they've finished their dance.'

The two horses were prancing around and the two men were having difficulty in keeping them from running off and leaving them treading on fresh air.

'Get them ropes off their necks,' snapped Nathan. 'Any silly tricks and you'll be burying yore boss.'

A Wolf and a Jackal

The men stared at their leader, waiting for him to make up his mind. They'd all scanned the rim but they could not see Nathan.

The man threatened, slumped in his saddle for a moment then he nodded. 'OK fella,' he called. 'You've got the drop for now so we'll do what you say. But don't think this is the end of anything. As long as you *hombres* are on my range this is only the beginning.'

The cowboys hurried forward, removed the lariats from the two men's necks and started to cut their bonds.

'Hold it,' shouted Nathan. 'Just cut the one with the fancy gear free. Leave the other one for now.'

Concho rubbed his wrists and began to turn his horse towards Nathan.

'Sit right there, *friend*!' snapped Nathan. 'Don't make me nervous 'cos you can die just as quick as the next feller.'

Concho half raised his hands. 'Aw come on now, Nathan,' he pleaded. 'I know I kinda played a trick on you-all, but don't be a sore loser, huh?'

'Get off the bronc, and make it this side so I can keep an eye on you.'

'You really are *the* most distrustin' feller I have ever met,' grumbled Concho as he slid obediently from the saddle.

'Hey, mister, did you say that hoss belonged to you?' called Nathan.

The stocky man looked up. 'That's what I said, stranger.'

'Then tell one of your men to collect it,' ordered Nathan.

'Hey,' protested Concho. 'You can't do that, Nathan. I own that nag, an' that's my rig on its back too.'

Receiving a nod from his employer, a cowboy stripped

off the saddle and bridle, dumped it on the ground and led the horse away.

Turning his horse towards the voice, the stocky man stared at the place for a few moments. 'This ain't gonna make no never mind, mister,' he said quietly. 'You may be an honest man, but hoss thieves ain't tolerated on this spread. We hang 'em. For now you've got a reprieve, but come sun-up tomorrow we'll be lookin' fer these two *hombres*. If we find 'em, we'll hang 'em. If you happen to be with 'em it'll be yore hard luck, you understand me?'

Without waiting for a reply he raised his hand and signalled for his men to follow him, as he spurred his mount and loped steadily out of the basin.

Eli had said nothing, and had not moved throughout the exchange. Now he stared at the rim, as if by his stare alone he could force Nathan to show himself. His hands were still tied but he sat his horse with the calm ease of his Indian forbears.

Concho was sitting disconsolately on his saddle. 'That was not a very smart move, Nathan,' he complained. 'You didn't even get our guns back from that thieving bunch; we'm worse off now than when we started.'

'You could have had your neck stretched instead,' replied Nathan dryly. 'Help Eli get down from his hoss, I ain't leaving nothing to chance this time.'

'You-all mean you ain't gonna shoot him while you've got the chance?' asked Concho in surprise. 'Whatever happened to family tradition? It must be way past time for one of you tuh shoot t'other.'

Eli, scorning any help flipped one leg over the side of his mount and slid to the ground with ease, as Nathan slowly made his way down from the rim.

'I saved your life Eli,' Nathan said as he approached. 'You owe me.'

A Wolf and a Jackal 95

'I owe you nothin' little brother,' spat Eli. 'If you think this lets you off the hook you'd better shoot me now.' His eyes seemed black with the intensity of his hate. 'I'll get you if it takes forever.'

Nathan stared at his brother as if mesmerized. 'I can't kill you Eli,' he muttered, 'you're my brother. I'm gonna leave you here to take your chances. When you get free of those ropes, go back home Eli; I don't want to have to kill you, but if I see you again I shall have no choice.'

Eli stood with his hands tied behind him, his whole body trembling with barely controlled hate. 'Run little brother,' he snarled. 'You ain't got the guts of a louse. Look over your shoulder an' I'll be there. Go to sleep, I'll be in yore dreams. I'm gonna kill you Nathan.'

He watched Nathan mount his horse and pick up the reins of the packhorse.

'Leavin' me afoot and tied too eh, Nathan? Well it won't make any difference.'

Concho had already thrown Eli's gear to the ground and replaced it with his own. He slid into the saddle, itching to be gone.

'Why don't you-all save yourself a lot of worry and plant a couple of slugs in him?' he snarled. 'We've got enough to worry about with that posse of ranchers on our tail without having to worry about him.'

'I can't kill my own brother in cold blood,' replied Nathan.

'OK, so give me the rifle. I'll do it.'

'There's only one gun between us an' I'm keeping that,' replied Nathan. 'Let's go.'

They backed away from Eli, then turned the horses, riding quickly into the forest.

'You know you should have shot him!' shouted Concho above the noise of the pounding hooves. 'He ain't gonna give up.'

'I'm hoping he'll remember that I saved his bacon back there and call it quits.'

'Man, are you a glutton for punishment,' replied Concho. 'Now me, I'd—'

'I *know* what you would do,' interrupted Nathan. 'Just be glad I'm not as vicious as you, otherwise the pair of you could have been swinging together from a cottonwood.'

'Yeah, OK, thanks for hauling our asses out of trouble. I'd go down on bended knee, but I don't think we're gonna have the time. Those *hombres* ain't gonna wait to start lookin' for us like they promised.'

'They're men of their word; if they said tomorrow that's when we can expect 'em.'

'It's Eli you should be worried about. He won't forget what you said about 'breeds.'

'Aw come on, he'll understand. I had to say *something*,' protested Concho.

'Like you said, Eli ain't too strong on *understanding*. He'll be along, so I reckon we should put as much space between him and us as possible.'

'Amen to that,' agreed Concho as he urged his mount to even greater efforts.

There was a sudden flurry of shots from behind. Nathan glanced quickly over his shoulder.

The posse of cowboys were back with guns in their fists.

Another volley, followed by the ominous whine of a bullet ricocheting off a rock made the two beleaguered men kick their mounts into a faster pace until they seemed to fly over the ground side by side.

'He said they wouldn't come for us until tomorrow, the lyin' bastard,' panted Nathan.

A Wolf and a Jackal

'You believed him? Dear simple Nathan, a babe in arms that's what you are,' replied Concho derisively. 'They should never have let you out into this big bad world all by yourself, old son.'

Suddenly Concho swerved his mount close beside Nathan. He leaned out and snatched the rifle from Nathan's grasp.

As he straightened up he flipped his foot from his stirrup and kicked Nathan viciously in the side.

Nathan gasped with pain at the treachery but managed to stay in the saddle.

His mount veered away and Nathan found himself riding away from Concho at an ever-increasing tangent.

Nathan had lost control of the horse but fought grimly to bend it to his will as it continued its breakneck run through the forest.

A low branch crashed into his chest sweeping him from the saddle sending him crashing to the floor amid an agony of pain.

Nathan groaned as he attempted to struggle to his feet. The pain in his chest seemed to lighten, and he dimly heard Sarah telling him she was sorry.

He opened his eyes, Sarah was leaning over him, staring worriedly into his face.

'Are you all right?' she murmured. 'I guess I rolled over on to your chest in my sleep. Sorry honey.'

Nathan grinned, and drew her to him. 'You can lie on *my* chest any old time, Sarah honey,' he replied. 'I guess my dreamin's over for tonight. Tomorrow we'll move into town and join that wagon train. We could maybe lose ourselves in the crowd, and once we start the trek into Wyoming territory with the wagon train, no one will know we were ever in Peaceful. Even Eli can't follow a trail if there isn't one.'

'It's the stuff dreams are made of, Nathan. Breaking new territory could mean settling down in a real honest-to-God house somewhere.' Sarah leaned over and kissed him. 'Don't misunderstand me, Nathan. I'll travel like this forever and be glad of it just to be with you but—'

'I know, I know,' Nathan interrupted her quietly. 'And who knows, there might even be time for us to add to our family; after all thirty ain't old is it?'

'Oh Nathan,' Sarah murmured, snuggling into his shoulders. 'It's a wonderful dream, I hope it comes true one day.'

'Me too honey. Go to sleep now, we'll be moving at first light.'

THIRTEEN

Sanchos Alvarez was sitting in a dark corner of the *cantina* where he was sure he could not be observed.

He was surreptitiously watching the grim form of Eli Kyle as he leant on the bar sipping a beer.

This one would be afraid of nothing, Sanchos told himself. Even the terrible sight of last night would not upset this halfbreed.

Sanchos gave an involuntary shudder at the thought. He could remember it so vividly, and the thumping of a major domo of all headaches did nothing to ease the churning of his stomach. He would offer the man $500 to kill the gringo. It would not do to offer too much he told himself. The man might feel that the job would be too difficult if the price was high.

He glanced up from under his sombrero again and tensed as he saw the halfbreed turn in his direction and begin to stroll across.

'Surely he cannot think that I am watching him,' Sanchos muttered.

Eli seemed to glide smoothly and silently across the floor, so that before Sanchos was fully aware of it, the man was leaning over him, the tips of his fingers taking his weight on the table, his impassive face within inches of the Mexican's.

'What's so interestin' about me *hombre*?'

'*Señor!*' ejaculated Sanchos, taken aback.

'You heard me, Mex. You bin starin' at me ever since I walked in here. Perhaps you don't like 'breeds, is that it?'

'Oh no *señor*, I was indeed looking at you, and for this I apologize, but I was only wondering if you would be willing to carry out some work for a poor Mexican.

'I would pay very well,' he encouraged, as he saw the look of doubt cross the halfbreed's face.

Eli slid into the chair opposite Sanchos.

The way he moved reminded the Mexican of a mountain lion, fluid, smooth and deadly.

'What kind of job did you have in mind, mister?'

'First, may I say with all respect that I know of your reputation as a bounty hunter *señor*,' replied Sanchos, his flattering words dripping honey. 'I am prepared to pay well for the services of a man with your great reputation.' He spread his hands wide in an expression of innocence. 'This *hombre*, a mere *chico*, *señor*, has been causing me much trouble—'

'So take care of him!' interrupted the 'breed.

'Alas, *señor*, I am no *pistolero*. With the rifle I am not so bad, but with the handgun I am hopeless and it would be less than honesty to kill such a *chico* with a rifle.'

A cynical smile flitted across Eli's face and was gone. 'You don't look the kind of *hombre* to be that particular. In fact I'd be prepared to bet there's a picture of you on a Wanted poster somewhere – if I was a betting man that is.'

Sanchos chose to ignore the slur. 'I would be prepared to pay, say three hundred pesos for such a service.'

'Pesos!' queried Eli disparagingly.

'No, no, *señor*,' replied Sanchos quickly. 'Good American dollars.'

A Wolf and a Jackal

'Try me with a thousand,' grunted Eli.

'A thousand!' Sanchos sounded outraged, and waved his hands in dismissal. 'I am sorry, *señor*, but it seems that we cannot do business.'

Sanchos placed his hands on the table and started to push himself to his feet, but Eli gripped the Mexican's wrist.

It seemed a casual move, but Sanchos could hardly stop himself from wincing as he was forced to sit down again.

'Don't be in such a hurry, mister.' Eli's lips smiled but his eyes were like flint. 'Why don't you tell me about this kid an' maybe we could come to some arrangement.'

'It is no use, *señor*,' protested Sanchos. 'We are too far apart; I could not meet such a price.'

The grip on his arm did not lessen. 'So tell me about it.'

Sanchos knew he had gone beyond the point of no return with the halfbreed, so he told Eli as much as he thought he should know about Jeff Mason.

The 'breed listened, seemingly without interest. 'So if I was to take on this chore, how far would I have to travel to find this Mason *hombre*?' he asked.

'That is the beauty of it, *señor*,' replied Sanchos triumphantly. 'The *chico* is even now on the outskirts of this very town! He has been wounded, and is travelling in a wagon with a man and a woman, so it would be no problem for one such as you.'

Eli's interest quickened at the thought that he did not have to go out of his way to earn the money the greaser was offering.

'Tell me about the man and woman he's travelling with. D'you reckon the *hombre* will cause any trouble?'

'Oh no, *señor*,' scoffed Sanchos. 'He is a very big man it

is true, an' wears a *pistola* at his hip but he is a man of the cloth—'

'You mean a preacher!' Eli's interest was at fever pitch. The grip he had retained on the Mexican's arm suddenly tightened.

Sanchos visibly winced. '*Por favor, señor*, you are in danger of breaking my wrist,' he gasped.

'This preacher feller! Is he a big Texican, say about six three or four?'

Sanchos nodded, his face reflecting the pain. '*Si, señor*. Please, my wrist.'

Eli ignored the plea. 'An' the woman is she a little slip of a thing?'

'That I cannot say,' Sanchos almost sobbed, as the vice-like grip tightened even more.

Eli suddenly released the wrist and Sanchos sank back into his chair with a sigh of relief.

The halfbreed seemed to be drifting somewhere far away. 'Got 'em!' he gloated. 'At last I've got 'em!' He seemed to shake himself back to the present, as if realizing for the first time that the Mexican was still sitting opposite.

'Tell yuh what, Mex,' he muttered. 'I'll take on this little chore, cost yuh five hundred though, an' I want the money up front an' no messing. You doublecross me an' you're dead! Do I make myself clear?'

'*Si, si señor*,' replied Sanchos hurriedly. 'I will have the money here for you within the next two days.'

'You said you *had* the money,' snarled Eli. 'Well! Have you, or haven't you?'

'It is in a safe place, *señor*,' replied Sanchos. 'You would hardly expect me to carry such a sum around with me in a town like this, I am not a fool, *señor*.'

'Tomorrow then,' snapped Eli. 'Now, tell me where I

can find the wagon.'

The morning sun was still burning off the overnight mist as Eli rode across the hardpan towards the stream where, according to the Mexican, the camp had been set.

There was no sign of it, and Eli cursed himself for having been so confident in finding his quarry that he had allowed a day to pass while he had waited for his money.

Eli rode steadily along the bank of the stream until he saw where the wagon had been. He dismounted and began to quarter the ground, carefully studying the size and shape of hoof and boot marks with equal concentration.

After a few moments Eli removed a thin black cheroot from his pocket, thumbed a match into flame and lit the cigar. He sucked the acrid smoke into his lungs to try to overcome the excitement he felt.

He'd seen the tracks before, many times over the years, and it lay there before him like a picture book. His eyes followed the twin wheel-marks of the wagon as it headed towards town. 'Better and better,' he gloated. 'I can take my own good time. If I can take his woman first I'll have him. He won't go anywhere without her. With any luck she could be the bait to catch my particular catfish. Then I'll make him scream an' beg. I want this to last a long, long time.'

There was more than a touch of madness in his eyes as he relished the thought of his revenge. Eli wiped the spittle from his mouth, threw away the cheroot and remounted.

He was going to take his own good time over this, he ruminated. The kid was a nothing! to be disposed of when he was good and ready, but Nathaniel! Well that was something quite different. Nathaniel was going to pay very dearly for the slaying of his father, very dearly indeed.

Eli touched spurs to his mount and began to follow the wheel-tracks at a leisurely pace, his mind so immersed in the fantasy of his revenge that he failed to see the two Indians watching him from the cover of the same rocky section where Sanchos had so recently hidden himself.

'The hunter carries the look of death; he follows the trail of Bear Claw's friend, he should be warned,' muttered one Indian.

'But they have gone to the town of the white-eyes in their wagon,' protested the other. 'We have been told not to go there.'

'True,' agreed his companion. 'We will consult with Bear Claw, he will decide.'

The two Indians remained in the shelter of the rocks until the man in black was out of sight, then quickly mounted their ponies and galloped off to their camp.

Eli Kyle continued to follow the wheel-ruts made by the wagon. He stopped well away from the large cluster of wagons on the outskirts of the town. He knew that he dare not risk going openly among so many well-armed people.

Townsfolk tended to mind their own business, unless they were directly involved. They were much more concerned with profits and generally paid other people, like sheriffs or marshals, to deal with people like Eli, whereas the people in the wagons were pioneers. They expected trouble and grouped together to deal with it. Even the kids carried their squirrel guns with an air of competence.

A Wolf and a Jackal

Eli rode slowly around the perimeter of the wagons. He counted over sixty, and as each man wore at least one side arm and carried a rifle, it represented more fire power than Eli was going to argue with.

He saw quite a few of the teamsters stop and stare belligerently in his direction although he was nowhere near the wagon encampment, so he slowly turned his mount and rode quietly towards the *cantina*.

At least he was sure his quarry was somewhere within that constantly moving group of wagons and it would be only a matter of time before he spotted Nathan. Even then he'd have to use all his guile if he wanted to avoid a showdown with all those people.

But he could wait. His time was near. What could almost be a smile flitted across his face at the thought. Only once in the past had he been this close to Nathan. It had been at Bull Run. It had been a hurried, desperate affair, and he was glad now that he had failed. This time he'd be able to savour every painful moment of Nathan's death.

FOURTEEN

When the two Indians returned to their camp and told Bear Claw about the unknown man he knew that Mason should be informed.

Amid many protests, he decided that he would make for the area where the wagons were collecting, so that he would not have to risk entering the town itself.

This would reduce the risk of him being recognized as a warrior Indian. So, leaving his distinctive headdress with his warriors, he wrapped a large blanket around himself and rode to the large rocky area some six miles from the town. He close-hobbled his horse in a small coulée and continued his journey on foot.

Bear Claw was aware that a few Indians lived within the town. People who would wait upon their white masters hand and foot to obtain a few of the white men's coins so that they could buy the devil drink called whiskey.

He felt reasonably secure wrapped in his blanket, and he was sure that it would not take him long to find the wagon.

He had never entered the town in the past, and was both amazed and disgusted at the perpetual noise and squalor of the place. Bear Claw gazed at the many wagons in despair.

A Wolf and a Jackal

He'd had no idea there would be so many, but after some hesitation he began to shuffle along with his head bowed as he knew the Indians who frequented the place behaved.

Bear Claw kept glancing quickly from side to side as he progressed, hoping to catch a glimpse of the wagon he sought.

Some of the sights were so bad that he became absorbed with them.

Two burly teamsters were hurrying through the compound, eager to pay a visit to the fleshpots of the town, when Bear Claw inadvertently stepped into their path.

It was hardly a collision, but the two teamsters stopped. One grabbed the Indian's arm. ''Ere you, what the hell do you think you're doing?' he snarled.

He turned to his mate. 'Bloody Indians, think they own the town now, don't care who they push around.'

'Yeah,' grinned his mate. 'Well, what say we teach 'im a lesson?'

He swung a meaty fist at Bear Claw who easily avoided the clumsy effort and at the same time, quickly twisted out of the other man's grip.

They were both surprised at the speed and ease with which the Indian had slipped from their grasp, and all would have been well if Bear Claw had made his escape.

But he was an Indian chief and his honour would not allow these men to go unpunished. His knife slipped into his hand almost in reflex. The teamsters suddenly realized that this was no westernized Indian who would bow and scrape to them.

Bear Claw crouched like a cougar at bay, his concealing blanket discarded. The knife gripped in his right fist was poised for the lethal upward thrust, as he waited for his enemies to attack.

The two men backed off. 'Gonna try tuh knife us were you, you sneaky sonofabitch,' snarled one.

'Well, we got the answer, mister,' grated the other, as they both reached for their holstered guns.

'Let's see yuh dance, Injun,' growled the first as he fired at Bear Claw's feet.

'Yeah, dance,' echoed the other, as he also began to shoot at the feet of the beleaguered Indian, who was desperately jumping around in order to protect himself.

Jeff Mason had been taking a stroll around the area with Nathan when he heard the shooting start.

As the first shots crashed out and people began to converge on the spot Jeff glanced at Nathan in silent question.

Nathan hesitated, then nodded agreement, and they both hurried towards the noise.

Nathan used his large build to force the crowd to give way and Jeff stayed close using Nathan to protect his injured shoulder.

Utter silence suddenly descended upon the crowd.

By common consent the crowd had left clear a large circular area around the three combatants.

It was clear to the teamsters that the crowd of would-be pioneers were not in favour of what was happening.

'Damned Injun tried to skewer us with that knife of his,' snarled one teamster.

'Yeah, an' we're gonna prove that the only good Injun is a dead un,' growled the second, as he raised his gun.

Both Jeff and Nathan had instantly recognized Bear Claw.

Jeff stepped ahead of Nathan, into the clear area beside the Bear Claw.

'Git outa the way,' snarled the teamster. 'This ain't no place fer a snot-nosed kid.'

A Wolf and a Jackal

'Put the guns down,' replied Jeff evenly.

Nathan stepped up beside Jeff. 'You heard him.' His hand was poised above his gun. 'Put the guns down.'

The two teamsters grinned. 'Seems like we've got the drop, mister, but if you-all fancy your chances—' He thumbed back the hammer – it was the last thing he ever did.

Jeff's hand flicked down in a blur of movement. The gun seemed to grow in his hand and explode in one sight-defying moment of time.

The bullet tore into the man's stomach, instantly paralyzing all movement. It smashed through his spine, bursting from his back leaving a hole as big as a man's hand. He was dead even before he began to collapse.

Jeff was no longer interested in the man. On the heels of the shot he was turning towards the other teamster, hammer already at full cock.

The man tried to raise his gun. It was a waste of time, the shot was already on its way.

It burrowed in under his chin and burst through the back of his head in a welter of blood and bone.

By the time the man started falling Jeff's gun was resting in its holster once again.

Total disbelieving silence greeted the incredible display of gunspeed for a few seconds, then a sound something like a sigh seemed to pass through the crowd. The people began to move forward, becoming restive.

'Listen to me, you good people.' Jeff's voice was strong and clear. 'Soon you will be crossing this man's hunting grounds.'

The restlessness began to ease.

'This is a good man; he was unarmed except for a knife against two men with guns. I believe you should see that justice has been done here. You surely cannot want this man and all his warriors as your enemies while you are on your journey, so I ask you to consider the consequences of any action you may want to take.'

Arguments began. There was muttering and some shouting. Through it all Jeff and Nathan stood beside Bear Claw waiting.

One man stepped forward and the noise in the crowd subsided.

'I'm the man responsible for the success of this here trek so I reckon I ought to speak my piece here and now.'

There were mutters of agreement. It seemed the crowd accepted the man as a leader.

'Now I gotta admit that you talk a bit like a shyster lawyer I once knew back East, but I also admit that it took guts to stand there an' take two of my teamsters out as if they were nothin'. I also reckon you wouldn't take a risk like that if you was even doubtful of the Indian feller in the first place.'

He walked slowly towards Bear Claw.

'I ain't able to speak yore lingo, feller, but I sure am sorry this fracas took place.' He stuck out his hand. 'Jake Cord's the name an' I'd like us to shake on it, mister,' he finished, glancing at Jeff enquiringly.

Jeff nodded, and quickly translated to the puzzled Indian the gist of the message. Then he stepped forward and shook hands with the man to show Bear Claw what was expected.

Bear Claw copied Jeff's actions then raised his hand in the sign of peace.

Cord grinned and returned the gesture, then turned to the crowd.

'If some of you would cart this offal away perhaps we could all git back to our chores. There's a lot to do an' not much time to do it in.'

A Wolf and a Jackal

The crowd began to disperse and the man turned to Jeff. 'Hope you'll be comin' along with us, son, I sure could use a man who can speak the lingo as good as you. Tell me, where the hell did you learn to draw iron that fast? I ain't seen nothin' like that in all my born days.'

'Me neither,' muttered Nathan.

'Let's just say I had a good teacher an' leave it at that,' replied Jeff grimly. Now, if you will excuse me Mister Cord, I'm just gonna walk and talk a while with Bear Claw. I'm sure he didn't come here just for the ride.'

'Sure son,' replied Cord affably. 'Hope to see you around.'

The crowd gradually broke up, and apart from a few surly comments from some of the teamsters the general opinion was that old Judge Colt had settled another argument.

Jeff and Nathan walked to the edge of the wagons with Bear Claw, who now carried his blanket over his arm.

'Why did you take such a risk, my friend?' asked Jeff in Siouan.

'I came to warn you of danger; there is a man dressed in black and riding a black horse following your trail. My braves believe he is bringing the spirit of death with him.'

'Can you describe him?'

Bear Claw gave a good description of Eli Kyle. By the time he had finished they were on the extreme outskirts of the wagons.

Bear Claw raised his hand. 'I leave you now, Mason. Good hunting.'

Jeff raised his hand also. 'I thank you and your braves, Bear Claw. May you too have good hunting.'

'What was all that about?' asked Nathan.

'Seems that burr under your sadle is a lot closer than you thought,' replied Jeff quietly. 'Man dressed in black and riding a black cayuse mean anything to you?'

'Eli!' ejaculated Nathan. 'He's here!'

'It's what Bear Claw came to tell us.'

'Damn him to hell! He's never gonna leave us in peace.' Signs of desperation picked at Nathan's voice. 'All these years, and he's still there just like he said he'd be.'

Nathan's hands were clenching and unclenching in his agitation.

'Care to talk about it? I'm a good listener, Nathan.'

'Let's sit a spell,' replied Nathan. 'I've got to unload to somebody before I come apart.'

So they sat, and Nathan told Jeff the whole sorry story of his life of running from the brother who wanted him dead.

'I've had my chances to kill him, but I just can't kill my own brother, Jeff, and that's the sorry truth of it,' he finished.

'Is that because you're a preacher?'

'Even that's a lie,' replied Nathan. 'I only started to wear the dog collar because it threw Eli off the scent for a couple of years. Then I found that people left me alone because of it, so I kept the collar on and we both keep up the pretence. You see when Eli snapped my finger it never healed properly. The joint stiffened up so I was never able to draw a gun with anything like enough speed to protect Sarah, and the collar acted as a sort of protection—'

'But he's here now,' interrupted Jeff. 'An' you're gonna *have* to take care of it.'

Nathan shook his head stubbornly. 'I couldn't even get close in a quick draw with him. You saw me back there, I didn't even get my gun out and it was all over.

A Wolf and a Jackal

'No I'm just gonna have to get the wagon and run again.'

'It's got to stop some time.'

'When I'm dead,' replied Nathan bitterly. 'I'll stay in the group for as long as I can. Eli won't dare come in there after me. First chance I get I'll break away and try to lose myself in the Wyoming territories.'

'You've got a rifle,' responded Jeff.

Nathan shook his head. 'I can't face him in a gunfight, and I can't lay in wait for him with a rifle. If only I had your gunspeed I'd walk down the street and face him right now, but I haven't.'

Jeff glanced at Nathan thoughtfully as they walked back to the wagon.

Jeff did not think of himself as a gunfighter. He just happened to be very good with a gun, and while he had no compunction against killing the people who had attacked his family he knew that he could not kill Eli Kyle, a man he had never even seen and had no real reason to hate.

It was up to Nathan to remove that particular thorn from his side, and Jeff could not do it for him.

'I'd appreciate it if you didn't tell Sarah about Eli. She figures we might have lost him in the Dakotas an' I don't want her worrying.'

Jeff shrugged. 'It's for you to tell, not me,' he replied. 'But yore gonna have to do somethin' soon, Nathan.'

'Yeah, I'm thinkin' on it. Maybe I ought to face Eli right here in this God-forsaken town of outlaws.'

'Sleep on it,' replied Jeff quietly.

'Yeah, I might just do that,' replied Nathan tiredly.

Their steady stroll back to the wagon did not go unnoticed. On all sides men nodded and smiled. The story of the shooting had already circulated around the camp, receiving added embellishments with each telling.

It quickly spread into the town and by the time it reached Sanchos Alvarez it bore no relationship to the actual fight.

The Mexican was not even sceptical. His superstitions allowed him to believe anything of the man he called El Lobo.

Sanchos only hoped that Eli Kyle had not heard the tale.

'*Por Dios*,' he muttered. 'If that one had heard of it he would demand much more than the five hundred dollars he has already received.'

Sanchos looked around at the other Mexicans in the *cantina*; perhaps he should spend a little more money and buy some extra insurance, he thought morosely. If he had to run it would be as well to leave a few sharp-shooters behind, just in case.

With this in mind he accosted the *patron*, and after a long discussion there was a chink of dollars which left the fat man behind the counter with a broad grin on his face, rubbing his hands with glee.

Sanchos looked around the room again before leaving, the men lolling around looked vicious enough for anything. He breathed a sigh, it had cost him even more dollars but at least he would no longer be alone. If the man he feared ever entered the *cantina* there would be at least five guns waiting for him, and surely not even El Lobo could survive that.

Sanchos shook his head sadly when he thought of the many men El Lobo had already killed. He knew why he still had his doubts in spite of the men he had hired.

FIFTEEN

Sarah was very relieved to see the two men return.

She'd heard the gossip and could hardly wait for them to tell her the truth, yet in the true tradition of a frontier woman she greeted them as always, with a few sarcastic remarks about dishes having to be washed while grown men gallivanted off.

Nathan seemed withdrawn and although Jeff kept the conversation going, Sarah quickly realized that something was bothering both men.

That night as Nathan snuggled Sarah into his shoulder he told her all about the gunfight.

'Two men dead!' she whispered, awed at the enormity of it. 'He was that fast?'

'You couldn't believe how fast,' replied Nathan. 'I didn't even get my gun out and it was all over. I tell you, honey, I've never seen anything so fast in my life. I wish I—'

'Don't wish any such thing,' Sarah cut in, knowing his thoughts. 'I think we might have lost Eli at last. That's what I'm going to pray for anyway.'

Nathan kissed her. 'You do your praying an I'll do the hoping. G'night, honey.'

''Night, Nathan, sleep well.'

Nathan lay staring into the darkness long after Sarah

had gone to sleep, trying to accept the inevitable.

Tomorrow he'd find Eli and kill him, he'd use his rifle and kill him from cover.

It wouldn't be fair, and Nathan knew that he would never be able to forget, or forgive himself, but it had to be done. Eli would stand no chance at all, but it was the only way they would ever be free of the devil who had haunted him since he had shot his father.

Nathan's eyes gradually closed and his mind took him back, back to that terrible time of the first Bull Run—

Nathan had joined the Confederate Army out of desperation to leave Eli behind at last.

He looked down the smoke-blackened slope. His breath was forcing itself out in quick gasps against the cordite-filled air.

Nathan's mind had been bludgeoned for hours by the screaming, tearing sound of the artillery. Yet even that was now dulled by the heartfelt screams of the wounded and dying.

A cannon ball screamed overhead from the Union lines and smashed into a group of his newly acquired friends. Bits of human remains showered around him as his mind desperately tried to come to terms with the awfulness that was Bull Run.

Nathan had been coaxed along by smart talk of the men of the Carolinas. Those at Fort Sumter had fallen over themselves to give up they'd said. If that was the best the Union could do we 'uns will have this li'l ole war finished in no time at all they'd boasted.

Nathan crouched close to a ground which burst apart under the mighty explosions of the man-made hell and trembled.

His musket was loaded, his bayonet fixed. He was

A Wolf and a Jackal

waiting for the charge of the Union hordes to sweep over him.

Beside him a young scared face stared up at Nathan. 'We'm gonna beat 'em all to hell, ain't we Nathan?' The high-pitched voice, almost cracking with fear, held a forlorn hope which was not expressed in the scared eyes of the sixteen year old.

Nathan squeezed the boy's shoulder. 'Be ready, young Dan'l,' he muttered, trying to stop his own voice from trembling.

There was a pause in the thundering din, and then they came. Union soldiers fresh from behind the lines laughing and shouting in the confidence of their massive superiority in numbers and artillery. They had not been bludgeoned into mindless stupidity for hours on end, and they were for the most part, as young and untried as their Confederate opponents.

The front line dropped to their knees and fired a volley, the men behind the barricades began to fall.

Nathan turned to tell Daniel to keep his head down, but it was too late. Daniel had a surprised look on his face and a third eye in the centre of his forehead.

He would not have to be afraid any more.

Nathan fired his musket and reloaded. We are a rabble, he thought wildly. They're gonna walk right over us.

He fired down the slope again. Then from behind him came the God-awful screech of cannon balls. Not one or two as it had been from the Union lines, but in a long, almost nonstop volley which turned the din that had gone before into a mere nothing. The banshee scream was almost enough to drive the mind into a dumb insanity.

The Union soldiers were no longer shouting and

calling to each other. They were screaming and groaning as they were cut down like chaff from the bombardment.

The Union line wavered, stopped and then, miracle of miracles, the tide had turned. The Union soldiers were now the rabble. They were running back down the hill, their numbers reduced by every ball that landed.

Nathan finished the laborious job of reloading his single shot musket as he heard the order to *Charge*!

He began to move slowly down the hill.

In front of him he saw a Confederate soldier deliberately kneel and cut the throat of one of the officers.

The man's hands searched quickly through the dead officer's pockets, transferring everything he found into his own.

Nathan watched disbelievingly as the man reached for another wounded soldier and began to search his pockets also.

Suddenly his eyes focused on the man's hat and the silver *conchs*!

Nathan had not seen this man for three years but the hat told him everything.

The noise he made cocking his musket alerted Concho, who spun on his heels, still in his crouched position, the knife poised for an instant thrust as he stared down the musket barrel.

'Well I do declare,' he shouted in surprise, a big friendly grin spreading across his handsome face. 'If it ain't my good ole buddy Nathaniel Kyle.'

He started to get to his feet as he was speaking. 'Tell me now, Nathaniel, ole buddy, how's the family feudin' comin' along? You put a bullet into that brother of your'n yet?'

A Wolf and a Jackal

The broad smile was belied by the eyes, crafty, calculating and ready to accept the first opportunity to leap forward.

'God damn Nathan ole son but there's a lot of money to be made in wartime don't yuh know. We should git together like the ole buddies we were.'

He thought he saw his opportunity and leapt forward.

The heavy musket ball crashed into his chest throwing Concho into a backward somersault. He landed among his own victims, as dead as he'd ever be.

Nathan stared down at him his mind attempting to come to terms with the continuous noise of cannon fire, and the awful screaming of the dying and wounded.

'We were never buddies,' Nathan muttered sullenly, his mind wrapped in the hell around him.

The buzz of displaced air near his head made him realize that he was standing in full view of the enemy and he dived to the ground as yet another musket ball thwacked into the tree beside him.

Nathan lifted his head above the pile of dead bodies, his only protection against the musket balls humming through the air like angry wasps.

He wiped a dirty hand across his equally dirty face. Tasted the harsh burn of cordite fumes on his hands and spat in disgust.

The Union soldiers were in full retreat, no match for the sudden reinforcements General Jackson had pushed into the fight to help Beauregard's beleaguered troops.

Nathan's tired eyes began to follow the antics of a man wearing a blue kepi on his head, and a buckskin bush jacket. He darted from body to body. He'd turn over each one that happened to be lying face down, study the face for a moment then move on.

Something about the man kept triggering his memory.

A Union officer ran up to the man, and by his gestures he was demanding that the man in the buckskin coat go down the hill and keep up with the retreating soldiers.

The man pushed the officer away and continued his search. The officer drew his pistol and waved it threateningly.

The man in the buckskin coat spun like a cat, drew his own piece and fired all in one fluid motion.

The deep hollow boom of the old Dragoon Colt registered instantly with Nathan, and without thinking he shouted, 'Eli!'

Eli Kyle had not heard the shout above the bedlam of the artillery. He whipped off the officer's gun belts and strapped them about his own waist, then proceeded to rob the corpse of everything else it possessed.

Something made Eli pause and look around.

Nathan had clambered to his feet and was frantically loading his musket.

He looked up, just in time to see Eli take careful aim.

Nathan dropped instantly to the floor as the Dragoon boomed and a huge piece of bark was gouged out of the tree he had been leaning against.

Eli raised the weapon he had stolen from the officer and fired six shots at Nathan before giving way to the advancing Confederate soldiers.

SIXTEEN

Nathan awoke in a bath of sweat, his whole body trembling. He stared into the darkness of the pre-dawn, his mind slowly firming on the idea that now was the time.

Either he or Eli would be dead before this day was finished, and now was as good a time as any.

Nathan tried to slide away from his wife without waking her but it was a waste of time.

'Early out, Nathan?' she asked quietly.

'Things to do, hon,' he replied evenly.

'Things?'

'Yep, men's chores. They can't be put off. Hush now, go back to sleep, honey.'

Nathan climbed from the wagon carrying his boots and guns. He slipped on his boots and buckled the gun belt around his waist and checked the Remington before slipping it into its holster. The Henry rifle received the same careful scrutiny.

As he started to move away Sarah called quietly, 'Nathan!'

He paused and looked back at the dark blob that was the wagon. 'Yeah, hon?'

'Whatever it is Nathaniel, be careful for my sake,' she murmured quietly.

'Sure hon. Go to sleep now huh?'

Sarah did not reply but Nathan was almost sure he heard a quiet sob as he slowly walked away into the darkness.

He was not the only one moving about in the pre-dawn chill. A frontiersman started his day early and already there was the smell of bacon cooking, and the sound of children being roused ready for the new day.

Jeff Mason watched as Nathan walked away then followed in his wake.

He had spent some time cleaning and preparing his twin Colt Frontiers just in case he might have need of them. The holsters were snugged down and tied so that there would be no drag if he needed the guns in a hurry. Nathan was a good man, and as long as it stayed one to one Jeff figured he'd stay out of it. But he'd tag along just in case.

Eli Kyle was also moving around early. Some sixth sense seemed to be telling him that today was going to be his day.

He no longer wore the distinctive black clothes. His shoulder-length black hair was tucked back out of sight under a wide sandy-coloured stetson which was pulled well down over his eyes, shading his face against curious stares. A wide bandanna was tied around his neck, pulled up as close to his face as possible as a further precaution against being recognized as a halfbreed.

He wore only one gun, the Starr percussion. His distinctive Le Mat was hidden in the pocket of the cord jacket. A pair of well-worn jeans and black riding-boots completed his disguise.

A careful study of himself in the cracked mirror in his room satisfied him that he could pass unnoticed in the

A Wolf and a Jackal

crowded area of the wagon compound.

Eli Kyle could wait no longer for his revenge. He intended to seek out Nathan's wagon, force Nathan to drive it into the badlands and kill everyone in it.

Eli slipped quietly down the stairs and let himself out of the *cantina* turning quickly into the side alley and losing himself in the early morning darkness, cutting across the back lots towards the wagon compound.

Eli moved slowly through the groups of families, always keeping well in the darker shadows. He had no idea which wagon was Nathan's and he had never even seen the woman. All he knew about her was that her name was Sarah. She was less than five feet tall and kind of skinny with it. Nathan would stand out like a sore thumb; a head taller than most men and built like a barn door.

Apart from all that he'd *know* when he was close to Nathan. He always had, so he moved slowly through the people depending upon his sixth sense as much as anything.

But he got lucky!

A small bird-like woman with her hair pulled tight back in a kind of bun was just getting into a wagon when another woman called out to her.

'Mornin' Sarah,' she called. 'All ready fer the big trek?'

'As I'll ever be, honey,' replied the woman as she disappeared inside.

The woman laughed as she passed Eli.

'Would that be Sarah Kyle, ma'am?' asked Eli, touching a hand to his stetson respectfully.

'That it would, mister,' she nodded cheerfully. 'Fine mornin' ain't it?'

'Indeed it is, ma'am,' replied Eli. 'A *very* fine mornin' indeed.'

The woman passed on and Eli studied the wagon with an intense feeling of satisfaction. He ran his tongue over dry lips. He could feel the heat of his sudden exultation spread through his body.

It was here at last. Eli's hand gripped the Le Mat in his pocket. In his mind's eye he could see the explosion of the twenty gauge shot-gun cartridge and the mess it would make of Nathaniel's stomach.

He moved swiftly to the rear of the wagon. If he could get the drop on the woman quickly enough Nathan would stand no chance at all.

The Starr slid from its holster with practised ease as he pulled back the tarp and stepped quickly up into the wagon, snapping the tarp closed behind him.

'Just stay quiet an' still,' Eli cautioned Sarah, as he pressed the gun into her side.

Sarah was stunned. Petty thievery was almost unknown within the members of a wagon train.

They would be travelling together for many months, and if one was ever found to be a thief a swift and terrible justice would follow.

'Where's my little brother?' The words struck a knell of doom in Sarah's heart.

'Eli Kyle!' The ejaculation was instant as she twisted to face the man who had caused so much fear in her life. 'It *is* you isn't it?'

'I told him I'd come,' replied Eli coldly. 'He's bin lookin' over his shoulder fer a long time now, lady. Today's his turn to die like my old man did; now just you call him in here.'

Sarah's indomitable spirit rose in defiance. 'I can't call him because he ain't here, an' even if he was I would never call him to his death.'

The gun gouged into her side. 'You'll call him or

you'll die right now,' snarled Eli. 'I've waited too long fer this day.'

'So shoot me and be damned,' Sarah snapped defiantly. 'What kind of man is it that makes war on women anyway? Only a dirty sonofabitch dragged from the gutter would threaten a defenceless woman,' she sneered. 'So go on, shoot me if that's what you want to do. You'll have every man on this wagon train here in seconds. In fact I might just as well start shouting right now if you're gonna shoot me anyway.'

Eli Kyle had not expected such a tiny woman to give him so much trouble.

He realized she was right. If he shot her the men on the wagon train would crucify him and he'd never get to fulfil his threat.

He had to shut the woman's mouth and quickly.

Almost without thought his clenched fist crashed into her chin and she slumped to the floor without a sound.

Eli was beginning to panic.

He glanced around desperately. A piece of rope and an old head scarf were lying on the wagon floor.

Eli quickly bound and gagged the woman and pushed her into one corner so that she would be out of sight if Nathan returned.

After a few moments thought he decided to try to move the wagon out of the compound. If he could get it away from the crowd somewhere, Nathan would have to come looking for it. Then he'd have him.

He refused to think of what would happen if Nathan enlisted the men to help him look for his missing wife and wagon. Eli only knew that this was his chance and he had to take it. Nathan had to die and if he had to use a woman to capture him, so be it. She could die too for all he cared.

Eli pulled his stetson lower over his eyes and stepped down cautiously from the rear of the wagon.

He glanced surreptitiously around. No one seemed to take any notice of him, they were all busy with their various chores.

The two horses were grazing nearby and Eli strolled over to them.

After playing with their ears and petting them for a short while he led them back to the wagon. Quickly hitching them up, he climbed into the driving seat, and with a flick of the reins eased them gently through the press of wagons to open ground.

Eli breathed a sigh of relief as he slowly left the other wagons behind and set a course for the rocky section a few miles out of town.

SEVENTEEN

Nathan could only guess where Eli would be staying, but he was sure that if he wasn't camping outside of town it had to be in the Mexican quarter.

His mind was made up, so carrying his rifle at the trail he strode boldly towards the only Mexican *cantina* in town.

One glance at the tie rail was enough. The beautiful black horse was there!

It was typical of Eli that he had not even stabled the horse. Nathan knew that, to Eli, all animals were replaceable and therefore expendable.

It was while he was staring at the horse that he became aware of a slight movement behind him.

He spun about in alarm, the rifle at his hip ready for instant use.

'Man that was real fast,' muttered Jeff in surprise.

'What the Sam Hill are you doin' here!' ejaculated Nathan. 'I almost shot you.'

'Damn right you did,' replied Jeff, still shocked at Nathan's speed. 'And I'd have deserved it for being so careless. I'd never have dreamed a man your size could move so fast with a rifle.'

'So what *are* you doin' here?'

'Just gettin' some air, an' you?'

'At this time of a morning?' replied Nathan sceptically.

'Some law about that in this town is there?' replied Jefff with a small smile.

'You wouldn't be wet-nursing me would you?'

'Nope, but it's always good to have someone watching your back. Is that his hoss?'

'Yep.'

'Fine animal; pity your brother can't treat it right. You goin' in the lion's den now?'

'I'm thinking about it,' replied Nathan soberly as he stared at the *cantina* door. 'You thinkin' of goin' in?'

'I'm here, so I might as well,' answered Jeff almost casually, as he nudged his guns into a slightly more comfortable position. 'You ready?'

'As I'll ever be,' grunted Nathan.

By tacit agreement they strolled into the dark interior.

Sanchos was just coming down the stairs as he saw the two men enter the gloomy room below. The Mexican sucked in his breath as he recognized Jeff Mason, and eased slowly back up the stairs without turning around.

He paused on the landing and stared down at the four Mexicans lounging in the bar area; there should be five, but perhaps the fifth one was outside, it could make all the difference, he thought hopefully.

Sanchos had given his villainous crew of assassins a full description of the two men and had agreed to give each of them a share of five hundred American silver dollars, with a further bonus of one hundred dollars for the man who actually shot Mason.

The gloom within the *cantina* put Nathan and Jeff at a disadvantage, but they had no reason to expect trouble from anyone except Eli Kyle, and he would want to take care of his brother personally.

A Wolf and a Jackal

They moved carefully up to the bar area where the fat *patron* was slouched in his usual position with his chair tilted back against the wall, his feet resting against the counter and his sombrero over his eyes seemingly half asleep. The relaxed half-asleep manner was deceptive.

Jeff Mason was standing about four paces behind his friend as Nathan tapped the barrel of the Henry rifle on the counter top.

The fat Mexican allowed his chair to drop on to its other two legs. The sawn-off, double-barrelled shot-gun concealed in his lap and covered by a serape swivelled towards the man at the bar.

Nathan was surprised but ready.

At the first sight of the shot-gun Nathan's rifle spat fire.

The Mexican still managed to get off a shot, but Nathan's rifle had already smashed across the shot-gun striking it downwards and to the side.

The sound of the shot-gun was like the crack of doom in the confined space, and it was quickly followed by a pistol shot from one of the four Mexicans scattered around the *cantina*.

Nathan felt the sting of the bullet as it burned across his thigh. He spun around and slipped into a sitting position, making himself as difficult a target as possible against the black background of the bar.

As he dropped he levered a second shot into the rifle and fired in one swift motion.

A gun clattered to the floor as his bullet found the shoulder of the one who had put the bullet across his thigh.

The man spat curses in his native tongue as he scrabbled along the floor for his weapon. The man had the gun now and he thumbed back the hammer.

Nathan took more care with his next shot and the Mexican sank to the floor choking as Nathan's bullet took him through the throat.

Jeff dropped into a gunfighter's crouch as soon as Nathan had fired the first shot.

He turned quickly on his heel to watch the two men behind him.

They were both making their play but they were sitting at tables, and this slowed their reactions for a vital second.

Jeff was still unable to use his right hand for a quick draw because of the stiffness in his injured shoulder, but the left one was equal to the occasion.

The gun leapt into his hand as if it were alive, and as it levelled in the direction of the two Mexicans the right hand flicked across the hammer spur, fanning off four shots almost as one.

The first Mexican received two shots within inches of his heart and crashed forward into the table without a sound. The second dived in desperation behind the upturned table as the other two shots punched out large chunks of wood around the edge of it.

Jeff allowed the gun to drop a trifle and fanned the remaining two shots into the centre of the table top.

The man was forced from his hiding place as the two bullets drove into his stomach.

Jeff dropped his empty pistol and drew his right-hand gun. Gritting his teeth against the sudden pain he threw the gun across to his good left hand.

As the gun landed in his hand he turned and shot with one continuous movement at the fourth man who had decided until this very moment, to wait his chance and maybe win the bonus offered.

He was just rising from behind his overturned table

A Wolf and a Jackal

intending to shoot Jeff in the back. He panicked as Jeff fired at him and his first shot went wild. His second hit the ceiling bringing down a shower of plaster as Jeff and Nathan fired together.

The combined force of the two bullets lifted the man into the air and threw him over a nearby table. He was dead before he hit the floor.

After the bedlam of gunfire, the silence seemed almost deafening as the two men hurriedly looked around for possible danger.

Sanchos had watched the slaughter from the balcony in stunned disbelief.

'*Por Dios*,' he screamed, without any thought of the consequences. 'It ees impossible. Can no one keel El Lobo Diablo?'

At the sound Jeff shouted, 'Sanchos!' and fanned off his remaining shots at the balcony.

Bullets spattered all around the Mexican, and for those few seconds he bore a charmed life as he dashed back into his room and grabbed his carbine before running to the window and jumping to the dirt road outside. Ignoring the outside staircase, and without even thinking about a possible injury, Sanchos threw himself into his saddle and spurred out of town as fast as his horse could take him.

'So, the *señor* is out of bullets at last.' The voice had an oily satisfaction to it. 'My good *amigo* Sanchos has placed a great price upon your head, *señor*, and now I find you alone, with no bullets left in your gun, and no one left to share this great prize with. I am indeed fortunate do you not theenk so?'

The fifth Mxican had been outside and had just entered the *cantina*. He had not heard the sharper crack of the Henry rifle, and he could not see Nathan who was still sitting on the floor behind the curve of the bar.

The Mexican moved slowly into the *cantina*. The shot-gun he was holding was centred on Jeff. A touch of the twin triggers and his victim would be cut in half. To make matters even better, he knew Jeff was unarmed.

'Am I not one very lucky fellow?' the Mexican boasted. 'With this, my beautiful gun, I shall earn six hundred pesos. Look at it, *señor*, my beautiful, beautiful gun.'

The shot-gun tilted upwards slightly as the Mexican showed the wondrous gun to his victim, and for that second Jeff was out of the direct line of fire.

That was the moment Nathan put a bullet in the centre of the Mexican's forehead.

But even so, the slight depression of the hair triggers fired the shot-gun. The charge crashed into the ceiling bringing down even more plaster.

'You kinda took yore own good time there, Nathan,' Jeff grunted, trying to cover the slight tremble in his voice with levity. 'Figured you'd dozed off there for a while.'

'How could anybody doze off with you making all that darned racket?' replied Nathan. 'Apart from the fact that I got singed by that Mex in the corner, of course.'

'Bad?' asked Jeff in instant concern.

'Bet I don't git the nursin' my Sarah's bin givin' you lately.'

'Jealous huh?'

'You bet your life.'

'We nearly did.'

'What?'

'Bet our life.'

'Uh huh. You gonna look upstairs fer that Sanchos fella?'

'Nope, he'll be long gone, an' you can bet your brother

ain't up there either, he'd have bin down here before this.'

'Looks like we both wasted our time. We'd best git back to the wagon an' see if my Sarah's got some breakfast ready.'

Jeff helped Nathan to his feet.

The wound was no more than a scratch but Nathan vowed he'd make the most of it when they got back to the wagon.

'How much sympathy you reckon that little nick's worth?' queried Jeff.

'Don't rightly know,' replied Nathan. 'But I'll play it for as much as it's worth. It's time you started doin' the chores anyway.'

EIGHTEEN

Eli Kyle drove the wagon into a small secluded arroyo where it was completely hidden.

After checking Sarah's bonds he climbed from the wagon then, leading the horses to the edge of a steep grass-covered bank, he set the brake.

Pulling a bunch of hay from the wagon box he scattered it over the bank so that the horses could feed without trouble. Eli knew he could not allow them to wander into the open where they might possibly be seen.

The chances were remote but Eli was determined not to spoil the opportunity of settling the score with his brother.

Eli had not made any plans when he had left the *cantina*, so his horse and gear had to be collected as fast as possible. He could not have foreseen that he would be lucky enough to kidnap Nathan's wife so easily. But he was certain that if he did not collect his belongings very quickly indeed, he would have to leave them behind, and he needed his horse for his escape after he had killed Nathan.

The more Eli thought about it, the more dangerous his position appeared. Kidnapping a woman in this man's country was bad. For a halfbreed to abduct a white woman was unthinkable!

A Wolf and a Jackal

To the men back at the wagon compound it would be a hanging offence, and the nearest tree would do.

Eli removed his bush jacket and stetson. He checked to make quite sure Sarah could not break free and after some deliberation, reluctantly removed his guns and stowed them away out of sight.

He started back to town at a steady dog trot he could keep up all day if necessary.

As he ran he was pleased to see that the wagon had left little or no trail in the hard-baked ground. With any luck he would be back within two hours. Trackers would soon find him but all he needed was enough time to prepare for Nathan.

Provided he was back with the woman before they found him he wasn't worried. They could have her back in exchange for Nathan and a free ride out. She was only a means to an end anyway, and they wouldn't try anything while he had her.

Eli slowed to a walk as he came to the edge of town. He was surprised to see a crowd gathering around the *cantina*.

At first he thought the alarm had already been raised and he was being hunted.

He approached with caution until he overheard two old-timers talking about the shooting at the *cantina*. Satisfied that he was not the centre of interest he hurried inside in time to see bodies being dragged from behind some tables.

Eli hurried upstairs to his room, collected his bedroll which contained his clothes and rifle, then taking a last quick look around to make sure he had everything he glanced out of the window to check that his horse was still at the tie rail.

It was, so he made his way cautiously to the stairs. He

controlled his urge to dash downstairs and ride away but he knew that people would notice and remember. Moving as swiftly as he could without attracting undue attention he left the *cantina*.

Strapping his belongings behind his saddle he mounted, allowing the horse to lope out of town at its own pace.

Nathan and Jeff had to push their way through an inquisitive crowd as they left the *cantina*. Men and women alike, were hurrying from the wagon compound to discover what the recent gunfire was all about.

They continued to ease their way through the thinning crowd within the compound heading for their wagon.

Nathan stopped and looked around, puzzled. 'Where the hell is the wagon?'

'It ain't here!' replied Jeff, also staring around in perplexity.

'I can damn well see that,' snapped Nathan, the sudden worry putting an unintended edge to his voice.

He saw a woman he recognized, bending over a bowl wringing out some clothes.

'Excuse me, ma'am,' he called touching his hat. 'D'you happen to know where my Sarah's taken our wagon?'

The woman looked up and wiped a sudsy hand across her forehead.

'Well yeah, I happened to wish her good day earlier on, and as I was passin' some feller asked if the wagon was yours, seemed to know yore wife's name. Asked me, "Was that the Kyles' wagon?", so I said it was an' he climbed into the back. A few minutes later the whole kit and caboodle was hitched up an' gone.'

The woman went back to her washing.

'You happen to see which way they went, ma'am?' Nathan's voice had a touch of fear in it.

'No, sir, I did not!' replied the woman, clearly indicating that she felt Sarah should have let her know. 'They just up an' left, Mister Kyle, and not so much as a goodbye.'

She stopped suddenly as she realized the implications. 'You-all mean you don't *know* where she's gone, Mister Kyle?'

'That's what's worrying me, ma'am,' replied Nathan grimly. 'She wasn't meant to be goin' anywhere.'

'That damned halfbreed brother of yours,' snapped Jeff. 'While we were looking for him he was coming here.'

'Let's get back to the *cantina*,' answered Nathan urgently. 'He won't leave his bronc behind.'

He turned and began hurrying back through the people, who began to realize that something was wrong. They started to collect around Nathan and the woman, plying them with questions.

The woman mentioned that the man was a halfbreed. The cry was taken up and word was quickly passed from one to another.

Jeff looked quickly around. His palomino was grazing on a small hillock a short distance away and he hurried to collect it.

His saddle was in the wagon but that would make no difference; he'd ridden bareback many times in his younger days and a hackamore would take him no time to make from any old piece of rope.

There was an angry muttering as the crowd began to understand what Nathan believed had happened to his wife.

The voices grew louder and men began collecting

rifles from their wagons as they followed Nathan back towards the *cantina*.

Wives began to shout barbaric advice – advice the men did not need – on how to treat the halfbreed when they caught him.

When Nathan arrived at the *cantina* surrounded by dozens of vengeful men carrying guns, Jeff was already there.

He slipped from the palomino as Nathan approached.

'He's long gone, Nathan,' Jeff said tersely. 'Seems we missed him both ways. While we were goin' back to the wagon he slipped in, collected his gear and his hoss. Somebody said they seemed to recollect an *hombre* on a black hoss riding off towards the river.'

'I don't care where he is,' snarled Nathan. 'I ain't gonna rest till I've put him where he has always wanted to put me.

'Get me to a stable Jeff, I need a horse *pronto!*'

Jeff slipped easily aboard his mount then offered his hand to Nathan, who mounted behind him.

Nathan looked down at the crowd. 'Be obliged if some of you would help me by riding out in search of any sign of my wagon. I don't ask you to get involved, but it would help if I knew which way to go.'

There was a chorus of shouts as the men hurried off, while Jeff kicked his mount into a trot, heading for the livery.

The stable owner was standing at the door when they arrived. He looked up expectantly. 'Help you, mister?' he asked around a large chaw of tobacco.

Nathan slid from the palomino before it had come to a halt. 'I need a hoss, saddled and ready to go,' replied Nathan.

'Rent or buy?' asked the hostler, spitting expertly into

a large tin he kept for the purpose.

'Rent,' replied Nathan tersely. 'An' make it quick.'

The man spat again. 'I don't do deals in a hurry, mister, like to dicker a little first. Say what was all that shooting I heard up yonder?'

'Let's get to it, mister,' interrupted Jeff tersely. 'We're in a hurry. 'Breed just kidnapped this man's wife.'

The man almost swallowed his tobacco. 'Holy Jesus!' he muttered as he turned and hurried into the livery.

He returned with two horses and a rifle. 'Here's yours, mister, ain't no charge.' He booted the rifle and swiftly mounted the second horse as Nathan also swung into the saddle, then the three men turned and galloped back to the compound.

The place was like a disturbed anthill as men rode out in all directions.

Jake Cord was on hand organizing the men as Nathan, Jeff and the hostler rode up.

'We'll find him in short order; there's some good trackers in my lot,' Cord said confidently. 'First sign of tracks an we'll hear a rifle shot. Then God help him because he'll sure as hell need all the help he kin get.'

The shot was not long in coming, and with one accord men wheeled their horses and headed pell-mell towards the sound, each trying to out-ride the other.

In spite of riding bareback and using a hackamore, Jeff was soon in the lead, followed closely by Nathan and Jake Cord.

Ahead they could see the man who had fired the shot. He was staring at the rocks, the rifle still in his hand as the riders surrounded him and drew to a halt, fighting to control their restive mounts.

'What have we got, Zac?' asked Cord, as soon as he was close enough to be heard.

'Reckon he's holed up in them rocks yonder,' replied Zac. 'Wagon tracks go in an' there's no other place to hide for miles in either direction.'

'Let's git 'im then,' shouted some of the men. 'What the hell are we waiting for?'

'He's got my wife in there with him,' replied Nathan loudly. 'I reckon we're gonna have to hold our horses until we find out what he's got in mind.'

'He's right,' shouted Cord over the noise. 'Now why don't you boys sort of move in closer to those rocks just to make sure he don't make a run for it. I can't see him drivin' a heavy wagon far into that kind of territory, so unless he's gonna leave the wagon and ride through on his own he ain't goin' nowhere. Like Nathan says, we're just gonna have to wait and see what kind of game he's playing. So close up now, we don't want him slipping away, do we?'

There were general mutters of agreement as the riders slowly edged forward towards the rocks.

NINETEEN

Eli was pleased to see the wagon where he had left it. A quick glance assured him that Sarah was still bound and gagged.

He could see that she had been trying to escape for some time. Sarah was no longer where Eli had put her but her efforts had been in vain.

Eli had never lost a prisoner in his life. Once he tied them up they stayed that way.

It was overpoweringly hot in the wagon so Eli reached forward and released her gag. 'You want a drink of water, Sister-in-law?' he asked tauntingly.

'If I did, would you give it?' Sarah replied without showing a sign of temper.

Eli nodded, surprised. 'Why, sure I would.'

'Then I would like one, please.'

Eli was nonplussed. He had expected her to rant and rave at him. He climbed from the wagon, fetched her a dipper of water and held it while she drank.

'Thank you, Eli,' she said quietly.

'You-uh, want some more?' he asked diffidently.

'No thank you, that hit the spot just right.' Her bright birdlike eyes were staring into his.

'What are you lookin' at me like that for?' he asked truculently.

'Why, I ain't looking at you like anything at all, Eli. You seem to forget we ain't never met before and as you said just now, I'm your sister-in-law. Don't you find it kinda curious us being kin yet never having met?'

'Can't say I've given it much thought. It's Nathan I want.'

'Why?'

'He's never even told you?'

'Oh sure, he told me all about killing Matthew Kyle, but that was a long time ago and from what I heard he deserved all he got.'

Eli instinctively raised his hand to hit her, his eyes wild. 'Don't you talk about my pa like that,' he snarled.

'You gonna hit me, Eli? A tiny woman like me all trussed up like a turkey ready for dinner? He was Nathan's pa too, d'you ever stop to think of that? Or what it cost him to have to shoot his own father?'

'Nathan's gonna die for it and you ain't gonna talk me out of it either,' replied Eli almost defensively as he lowered his raised hand.

'Ain't tryin' to. Nathan could have shot you many times over, Bull Run for instance? And that time with the cowmen, you know that don't you?'

'Sure, I know, but he was too soft.'

'Or perhaps he loved you because you were his brother; you ever think of that Eli?'

'Nobody loves a halfbreed, lady, an' I should know.'

'The name's Sarah, call me Sarah, Eli. Did you ever *try* to let anyone love you?'

Eli stared sullenly at Sarah, his mind in a turmoil.

She wasn't knee high to a grasshopper yet she was trying to tear his whole life apart in a few moments. No wonder Nathan wore a dog collar, he thought wildly.

'Have you Eli?' she asked quietly.

He was confused, she'd broken in on his thoughts. 'Have I what?'

'Ever allowed anyone to love you, anyone at all?'

She was at it again, he thought. Well, he wasn't about to weaken. 'Paw did,' he replied hesitantly. 'He came for me when I was just a kid an' carried me away from the Indians; he didn't leave me behind did he!'

'But he killed your mother. If he really loved you he wouldn't have done that, would he? If he really loved you he would have stayed at the Pawnee camp and the three of you would have grown up together.'

Eli was becoming angry. 'That's enough. I'm not going to hurt you, ma'am — Sarah — but I've got to keep my vow. Nathan will come here for you. It won't take him long to find us. Then I'm gonna kill him.'

Eli picked up his holstered guns and strapped them on.

He showed her the Le Mat with its shot-gun under-barrel. 'I wanted to take him with this, but I'm gonna have to settle for the Starr,' he said almost conversationally.

He began to clean the guns and check the ammunition. He showed her the heavy gauge shot-gun cartridge before inserting it. 'You never know I still might get a chance to give him this before he dies,' he muttered.

'You know the others will come with him and they won't let you get away with this, don't you Eli?' Sarah persisted.

'Yeah I know, but I've bin in tight spots before. I'll wriggle out of it somehow.'

Eli undid the ropes around Sarah's ankles. 'Come on, we have to climb to the top of that rock over there so that when the posse comes they'll be able to see us.'

'You're so sure that you'll beat Nathan, aren't you, Eli? But suppose he wins?'

'He won't win,' replied Eli as he helped her climb the rocks. 'Nathan knows I can beat him, always have.'

'Not always. Remember when he beat you in a fist fight? You thought you could beat him then but you didn't.'

'Now look, lady—'

'Sarah, call me Sarah, Eli,' she panted as she continued to climb.

'OK, *Sarah*!' he capitulated. 'I don't want to hear any more. I just want you to button your lip, otherwise I'm gonna have to gag you again, understand?'

'Yes but—'

'No buts, Sarah; you ain't no-but a slip of a woman, but yuh sure can flap your lip an' no mistake. How Nathan puts up with it I don't know; he must be some kind of saint, or he's just as soft as he ever was.'

They had reached the top by this time and were both surprised by the large number of men congregated below.

'You ain't never gonna get away from that lot, Eli,' muttered Sarah.

'I said shut it,' he growled.

It was ominous to Eli that the large crowd of men had made no sound when he and his prisoner had appeared on the top of the rock. To his way of thinking they should be shouting and screaming oaths at him. An angry man is usually a careless man, and it gave a body some room to manoeuvre, but the crowd below seemed calm, and quietly very determined that Eli would not escape them.

'Can you men hear me?' he shouted.

He heard a muttering by way of reply, then a man who seemed to be a leader rode forward.

'My name's Cord. We hear you mister, and I'm here to tell you to let that lady go right now and you just *might* live to see another sunrise.'

'I don't aim to hurt the lady,' shouted Eli. 'Is Nathan Kyle down there?'

Nathan rode forward. 'I'm here, Eli.'

'You know what I want Nathan, just me an' you facing each other. I don't much care what happens to me after that. What do you say Nathan, still scared?'

'No, I ain't scared Eli, you may kill me but if you harm one hair of Sarah's head there's someone here who will hunt you down if it takes forever.'

Jeff rode out of the crowd and stopped beside Nathan.

Eli could see that Jeff was riding Indian style; he'd heard the tales about this kid, and knew he was the one the Mexican had wanted him to kill.

A niggle of worry pulled at him but he shrugged it off. 'The kid don't worry me one way or t'other Nathan. It's you I want. Will you meet me?'

'And Sarah?'

'Nothin' will happen to her if it's fair and square, you got my word on it.'

'I'll meet you, Eli.'

'I'm going back down now,' shouted Eli. 'I'm takin' Sarah to the wagon, but if I so much as see anyone crawling around in these rocks I'll kill her! You understand me?'

'I understand, Eli.'

Nathan watched helplessly as Eli and Sarah left the rock.

His eyes were like flint as he rode slowly back to the posse. 'I reckon you men might as well return to the wagons. I don't think Eli's gonna harm my wife and I wouldn't like her to be hurt by accident. I'd like to thank you-all for helping me find 'em so quickly, but I reckon it's my chore from here on in.'

The men nearest nodded in agreement. They could understand how it had to be so, one by one, they turned their mounts and rode away.

Jake Cord was one of the last to leave. 'You watch him like a hawk, Nathan,' he said seriously. 'I wouldn't trust that sonofabitch one tiny inch. He's a snake, make no mistake about that.'

'Thanks Jake,' replied Nathan. 'I'm obliged for all your help. I don't think Eli will harm Sarah; he knows he can beat me easily with a sixgun so he won't worry about losing. If he should break his word I know Jeff here, will take care of it.'

'Goes without sayin',' replied Jeff succinctly.

Jake nodded his understanding as he turned his mount and single-footed away.

Many thoughts chased each other through Nathan's mind as he watched Jake ride off.

He had no doubt about the outcome; he was willing to pay the price if it meant Sarah would be able to ride away unharmed.

He smiled rather hopelessly at Jeff. 'Looks as if my time's about come. The burr under my saddle has become just too much to put up with any longer.'

'I don't think you've thought this thing through,' replied Jeff. 'You've been running so long you've kinda forgotten that you might win.'

'There's no way I can ever beat Eli.'

'That's because you've come to think that there's only one way to fight him,' responded Jeff.

'There is!'

'You don't *have* to do it his way, Nathan.'

'What other way is there?'

'You remember I told you about Eagle Eye? Well, he was a very wise man. I mind a thing he once said to me when I was just a young shaver. He told me, "A man's a fool to fight a bear with a bear's claws or stand in front of a charging buffalo in order to stop it because he'll always lose".'

'Is that supposed to mean something?' asked Nathan sceptically.

'Yep; as I see it Eli is very good with his pistols, right?'

'Right!'

'But how is he with a rifle?'

'Eli won't go for that; he'll want to use his sixgun.'

'But that don't mean *you* have to use a sixgun, Nathan. I've seen you with a rifle and you'd be a match for anyone.'

'Close up, Eli would still dust my tail.'

'Of course he would, but if you stay at extreme pistol range he can't just draw and shoot. He's gonna have to aim and that takes time.'

'You mean—'

'Right!' interrupted Jeff. 'He can use what the hell he likes but he ain't gonna be any faster than you, and he sure-God can't shoot any straighter. You got the beating of him with that Henry rifle of yours every time.'

'That friend of yours was some smart Indian,' grinned Nathan, relieved. 'At least it gives me a fighting chance.'

Nathan offered Jeff his hand. 'Sure was a damned lucky day for me when we rode along by the Dust Bowl, son.'

'For me also,' grinned Jeff, as he shook Nathan's hand. 'I think it's time to give Eli the chance he's been waiting for all these years, don't you?'

'Yeah, but I have to say I *still* don't relish the idea of

killing my own brother.'

'You just keep on thinkin' of Sarah,' Jeff replied grimly. 'I always thought about my folks every time I began to weaken.'

Nathan sighed. 'You're right of course, and the quicker it's done the sooner Sarah an' me can settle down to a real life somewhere – if I win.'

TWENTY

Eli felt a grim satisfaction as he helped Sarah back down into the arroyo and led her towards the wagon.

At last he was going to fulfil his vow. Very soon now Nathan would be dead.

'Can't you even untie my hands?' panted Sarah as he bundled her unceremoniously into the wagon.

'Not likely, Sarah ma'am, you-all is about *the* feistiest little lady I've ever laid eyes on in all my born days,' replied Eli. 'Why, I wouldn't put it past you to go for me with your teeth and nails if I gave you half a chance, and I've waited too long for Nathan to face me in a showdown to make any slip-ups now.'

Eli climbed into the wagon and retied Sarah's ankles, then taking another piece of rope he slipped it through her bonds and tied it to the side of the wagon.

He stepped back to admire his handiwork. 'You ain't goin' nowhere, Sarah, and I ain't gonna gag you because I figure that if you shout your head off Nathan will come just that much quicker.'

He unrolled his bedroll and removed his clothes, dusting them off carefully as he laid them to one side.

'What's with the clothes?' asked Sarah, curious in spite of her predicament.

'Them's special, Sarah,' replied Eli almost reverently.

'Them's my killing clothes. I'll just step outside to put 'em on, then you'll see why they call me *Death*!'

Eli stepped down from the wagon and stripped down to his longjohns, then carefully slipped on the black trousers. The waistcoat came next followed by the black bootlace tie. Eli combed his black shoulder-length hair, then carefully placed his black Amish hat on his head and slid the black bootlace chinstrap tight under his chin. Last of all he strapped the two guns around his waist.

He made several practise draws with the Starr and followed this with secondary draws with the Le Mat. Eli was ready!

Sanchos watched Eli prepare himself for the fight with bated breath. Of all the places to hide his money, he thought dolefully, it *would* have to be in the very arroyo where Eli Kyle chose to have his final showdown with the man Sanchos now knew to be his brother.

After the shooting in the *cantina* and his close brush with death, Sanchos had only one thing in mind, to collect the money from its hiding place and ride for the Rio Grande.

True it was a very long way from the badlands of South Dakota to El Paso, but nowhere could be too far to get away from the man he feared more than anything in the world. But for now he had to hide and wait; maybe in the end he would manage to escape, anything else was unthinkable! Sanchos shivered at the possibility.

He watched as the man in black walked slowly to the rear of the wagon and pulled back the tarp.

Slowly and silently, almost as if he had risen from the depths of the earth, Sanchos saw Jeff Mason appear about twenty feet in front of him, close to the horses.

His eyes widened in disbelief, and he instinctively reached for his machete. It was easy throwing distance and Sanchos was an expert.

He paused knowing the noise would alert the man in black. Sanchos glanced quickly at Eli and back again.

His nemesis had gone! Disappeared as silently as he had arrived. Or was he ever really there? Sanchos asked himself.

'I'm ready to keep my vow,' Eli told Sarah rather portentously.

Sarah stared back boldly at him but in her heart she had to admit that the very sight of Eli dressed as he now was put the fear of God into her. He was so confident she thought desperately, that she had to try to shake him. To make him unsure somehow. She forced a smile.

'You're getting to believe your own hex, Eli,' she said, the hint of a sneer in her voice. 'Those fancy clothes don't make a damned bit of difference; a bullet will still leave you just as dead whether you're wearing 'em or not. It will take more than that to worry my Nathan.'

He leaned forward as if to say something to her but he was interrupted by a shout from the other side of the arroyo.

'Well Eli, I'm here,' Nathan shouted.

Eli twisted on his heels, eyes squinted against the sun's glare, searching, hands poised over his guns.

'I don't see you Nathan, is this some kind of trick?'

'You know it ain't, Eli. Stand away from the wagon.'

Eli had the spot placed now. He stared hard at the rock where Nathan was hiding.

'Show yourself, Nathan,' he called.

'Move away from the wagon,' Nathan repeated, 'You know where I am, or are you scared of *me* now, Eli?'

The rock was at extreme pistol range so Eli began to

move slowly towards it, poised ready for instant action.

'Remember Nathan, you try anything sneaky and I'll kill that wife of yours. I've got her strapped to the side of the wagon. I know just where she is: one bullet an' she's dead.'

Eli continued to pace slowly forward as Nathan slid from behind the rock.

Eli saw the rifle!

'What the hell are you playing at Nathan!' he shouted.

'You said you wanted to kill me,' replied Nathan as he slowly crouched, placing the rifle carefully on the ground and putting his hands on his knees. 'Your best way against mine, Eli. Any time you're ready.'

Eli stopped, undecided, the initiative had been taken from him. This was not the way he had planned it.

'You doublecrossing swine,' he snarled, the beginnings of fear etching his voice. 'I told you I'd put a bullet into the wagon if you didn't play it straight.'

'You'd never make it, Eli, and this *is* straight. Your fast draw against my rifle.'

Eli rubbed his hand against his trouser-leg, showing his nervousness; he felt sweat trickle down the back of his neck as he began to ease forward.

'Far enough Eli!' snapped Nathan.

Eli heard the wagon start to rumble away. He desperately wanted to turn around but he dare not take the chance.

It was a long pistol shot to where Nathan was crouching and Eli knew he would have to take time to aim.

'Spit or close the window, Eli!' Nathan snapped. 'We've both got an even shake.'

With an animal-like howl Eli raced three paces and dragged iron as he threw himself flat on the ground to make the smallest possible target for Nathan to aim at.

A Wolf and a Jackal 153

The Starr was pointed in front of Eli giving him the maximum chance to aim.

As Eli charged forward Nathan dived for his rifle. Lying on his stomach he rolled quickly sideways, rifle coming on target.

The Starr spat flame and Nathan felt a searing pain along the side of his leg as the bullet sliced through his jeans. The next bullet cut across the top of his shoulder. An inch to the left and it would have entered his skull.

Nathan rolled quickly to his left and two more slugs spat dust from the place he had been a moment before.

The rifle centred again and Nathan squeezed the trigger.

Eli grunted with shock as the slug burrowed into his shoulder. Suddenly his nerve broke and he tried to scrabble to his feet.

For the first time Nathan could see more of Eli than part of a face behind a sixgun. By attempting to get up Eli had unwittingly exposed his chest.

Nathan centred on the target. Two puffs of dust spurted from the black coat. Eli staggered almost upright as two more bullets smashed in just above the heart.

It was as if Eli had run into a wall; the shock of the bullets held him upright for a few heart-wrenching seconds before he suddenly crumpled into the dirt.

Nathan threw the rifle from him and ran towards his brother. There were tears in his eyes as he put his arms under Eli and lifted him gently.

Eli's eyes opened, there was a trickle of blood from his mouth. He looked up.

Nathan was shocked at the sheer raw hatred he saw there. Hatred, and something else too. A kind of unholy gloating joy.

Nathan felt the press of the Le Mat in his side.

He could do nothing! His hands were wrapped around Eli and he was helpless!

As if in a dream he saw the barrel of a 30.30 pushed into Eli's face.

The noise was like the crack of doom and Eli's face disappeared in a welter of blood and bone.

The pressure of the Le Mat fell away from his side and Nathan looked up to see Sarah standing there with the carbine hanging from one hand.

'How did you know what he'd do?' Nathan asked, still dumb with shock.

Sarah shrugged. A weary, hopeless movement of complete dejection. 'I remembered about how he broke your finger by pretendng to be unconscious when you were boys, Nathan. I wasn't about to let it happen again,' she said tiredly, offering a wan, miserable smile.

Nathan allowed Eli to slip from his arms. He slowly stood up and wrapped them around Sarah, pulling her close, holding her so tightly that she was almost gasping for breath.

'How?' he asked, still dumbfounded.

'Jeff cut the ropes with that knife he carries around his neck,' she explained. 'He didn't know that I grabbed the carbine and slipped off the back of the wagon while he led the horses away. I was determined that even if Eli won, he'd never live to gloat over it.'

Nathan kissed her long and hard before reluctantly releasing her.

'So you never did kill Eli on your own, Nathan, we did it together,' she murmured.

She started to cry then and Nathan tried to comfort her.

'I'm so sorry, honey,' he murmured. 'This should

A Wolf and a Jackal

never have been your fight.'

'It's always been our fight, Nathan,' she replied, still sobbing quietly. 'I'm not sorry he's dead. It means it's over at last. There was no forgiveness in him and I don't have any regrets about helping to kill him.'

From his position near the wagon Jeff could see that Nathan and Sarah needed privacy just now, so he slipped away and collected the horses they'd left outside the arroyo.

By the time he returned they had composed themselves and Nathan was rolling a quirley.

'That Indian friend of yours knew what he was talkin' about,' grunted Nathan. 'As it was Eli had four chances at me before I could get off a shot; it was the distance that counted in the end.'

'You want a hand with the burying?' asked Jeff as he dragged his saddle gear from the wagon and began to prepare his mount for the ride into town.

'We'll see to that later,' answered Nathan. 'Me and Sarah have a whole new life to plan for, and we aim to give it some thought for the next hour or so. Right honey?'

Sarah nodded, she was still too full to speak.

'You've still got Parker Rivers' sawn-off and Kincaid's sixes in the wagon, Nathan. There's a two-thousand-dollar reward on each of those two I'm told. Make a great start to a new life.'

'That's yours,' Nathan protested.

'If you was to take 'em to Casa Verde you could collect the reward and tell the marshal that I'm still hunting his dinero. Make him understand I didn't steal it. You'd be doing me a big favour, Nathan.'

They shook hands. 'You're going back to town after that damned greaser.' Nathan made it a statement. 'You want company, you've only got to say.'

'My chore,' replied Jeff evenly. 'Look to see you both in the wagon compound later.' He touched his hat. 'Bye, ma'am, see you in town.'

'You'll wait for us there, Jeff,' called Sarah, as he spurred away. 'Don't go running off before we say a proper goodbye, you hear me!'

Jeff lifted a hand in acknowledgement as he rode out of the arroyo.

Nathan and Sarah watched Jeff until he was out of sight then climbed slowly into the wagon.

'Don't hardly seem real,' Sarah sighed, as she sat beside Nathan.

'Yeah, an' it took a smart young fella to show me how I could tackle Eli fair and square, and still beat him.'

Nathan dragged the sawn-off and the matching sixguns from the cupboard.

'They're worth four thousand dollars to us in Casa Verde,' muttered Nathan. 'Just think, gal, that's over six years' pay. We could buy a small farm with it and start our lives over.'

They sat together on the inside wagon seat where they had spent so many hours in the past. Nathan gently kissed Sarah.

They leaned back into the canvas side of the wagon as they had done so many times before. Nathan slid his arm around Sarah's shoulders as they silently contemplated their new life together: a life without running; being able to live as they had always wanted to live.

Nathan gave Sarah's shoulders a companionable squeeze. 'Reckon there won't be any bad dreams from now on Sarah, honey,' he murmured in quiet satisfaction.

TWENTY-ONE

Jeff was riding out of the arroyo when he noticed some horse droppings in a small cut-off close to the main trail.

On an impulse he reined in and dismounted. Leading his own mount he began to follow the tracks.

The sides were smooth and sheer. Jeff released the reins and began to move swiftly but cautiously along the narrowing trail.

He heard the stamp of a hoof ahead and the gentle blowing of a horse.

Jeff slid quickly around the bend in the trail into a box canyon. He saw the horse, untended, snuffling through the sparse grass. Jeff's eyes quickly scanned the sheer cliffs; there was no hiding-place there.

His mind clicked, Sanchos! He was here! But not with his horse, so where?

The wagon! On the heels of the thought Jeff began to run back the way he had come. Sarah and Nathan were back there, and they had no idea that the murdering Mex was anywhere near.

Outside the wagon Sanchos saw the twin bulges in the canvas as Sarah and Nathan relaxed against it.

$4,000! He tried to shut it from his mind. But it would be so easy, the insidious murmurings of his greedy mind prompted as, almost without thought, he drew his pistol.

Señor Mason will be well out of earshot by this time, his mind coaxed temptingly as he raised the pistol close to the revealing bulges in the canvas.

Just two shots, then he could collect the guns and hurry to that other cache so close to where Eli Kyle was lying. He would be gone in moments.

He eased back the hammer.

Jeff's voice sounded like the call of death as he yelled, 'Sanchos!'

The Mexican stared disbelievingly as Jeff thundered across the arroyo on his devil horse.

In automatic reflex Sanchos fired at the charging figure before dashing into the rocks for cover.

Jeff hit the ground running, his Colt already jumping into his hand and sending bullets humming into the niche where Sanchos had taken cover.

With no thought of danger Jeff charged into the opening but it was empty.

Some stones and rubble rattled down from above and Jeff had a momentary glimpse of a pair of boots as they disappeared over a ledge.

Sanchos was climbing on trembling legs; he had no thought of returning the shots. He was already convinced there was nothing he could do against this devil, all he wanted was to get away and hide.

Jeff climbed as rapidly as his weak shoulder would allow. More stones fell around him and he caught brief glimpses of the Mexican as he climbed, but his weak shoulder would not hold him, neither could he use the arm to fire his pistol so he just kept climbing.

Sanchos grabbed a huge boulder in his frantic climb; it was loose. He looked down. Jeff was directly below and closing fast.

Sanchos climbed above the boulder and began to rock it with his foot. Slowly it tilted outwards sending a shower of debris in front of it before almost lazily rolling from its place.

The shower of stones warned Jeff. He glanced up to see the boulder toppling towards him.

In desperation he jammed himself into a small crevice as the boulder passed over him.

As the dust cleared Sanchos was horrified to see his nemesis still climbing.

'Nothing can stop him,' he sobbed, as he continued to scrabble upwards.

Suddenly there was nothing in front of him, just a gaping chasm.

With a squeal of terror he turned and began to empty his gun at his enemy.

With bullets buzzing around him, Jeff knew he had to fight so, hanging on to the rock with his good arm, he used his injured one to draw his gun. Grimacing with pain he fired twice and was rewarded by a high, piercing yell.

He looked up but Sanchos was no longer there.

Jeff quickly climbed the rest of the way. A gun and a sombrero lay in the rocks. He leaned over the chasm. It was a long way down. There was a splash of blood and a deep gouge where rocks had been displaced.

Jeff was almost overcome by vertigo as he leaned far out to try to see where Sanchos had fallen and he was rewarded by signs of blood further down.

Jeff felt an emptiness deep inside him. It was over at last, he thought remotely. No one could fall into that chasm and walk away. He threw the gun and sombrero over the edge.

He didn't hear the gun hit bottom and the hat floated

lazily from side to side for a long time before it eventually disappeared.

The money would probably never be recovered but at least Nathan and Sarah would go to Casa Verde to clear his name thought Jeff as he slowly descended to the arroyo. Maybe one day he'd look them up on their farm, but for now – well he still had a lot of riding to do, and places to see before he settled down.